Bones of the Woods

A collection of short stories
by Rachelle Reese and John E. Miller

ISBN: 1-4196-7059-X
ISBN: 978-1-4196-7059-6
Printed in the United States of America

Acknowledgements

Rachelle's acknowledgements
So many people have helped me grow as a writer and as a person that I cannot list them all here. However, I would like to acknowledge those who have done most to make me who I am and to make sure this book saw the light of day. First, I'd like to thank John for pushing me to get the final touches done, even though the demands of work made it hard sometimes. I'd also like to thank my parents for raising me with the belief I could do anything I put my mind to, the understanding that true success requires hard work, and the courage to pursue my dream of being a writer. Finally, I'd like to thank my friend Cousette Copeland, who helped me let creativity flow back into my life and encouraged me throughout the process of writing these stories.

John's acknowledgements
I would like to first to thank the storms of 2006; if it wasn't for them this book might not have been written. I would like to thank the people I game with; without them I'm afraid I would lose my imagination. I would like to thank my mother and father. First, if it was not for them I would not be here. Second, they showed me how to love this world we live in. I dedicate my part of the book to my father, Lee Miller. He showed me that you fight a good fight even when you know that you're going to lose. I would like to thank the rest of my family because without them I would have a dull life. Finally, I would thank my wife, Rachelle. Without her I truly would not be in this world right now. We have seen the worst of times and best of times, but baby we made it this time.

Contents

Copyright © 2006 Amanda Hopper

Forward

By Rachelle Reese

We will forever remember 2006 as the year of the storms. The first storm, short-lived but violent, struck when the new leaves were just beginning to open on the trees. John and I had gone to the grocery store in a nearby town. As we walked through the aisles of the store, the intercom warned of tornadic winds, lightning, and hail. The sky darkened as we filled up the tank with gas and headed home. We turned off the highway onto the country road that leads to the dirt road we live on. As we drove around a curve, John slammed on the brakes. A large tree blocked our path. We assessed its size and decided we would go the other way. John turned around and headed up the highway. When we reached the turnoff for the road that would lead us to our house, we noticed a truck stopped at the corner. The driver was waving his hands. "There's a tree up there. You can't get through," he said.

"How big?" John asked.

"Big," the man said. "If you want, go up and take a look. If you can get around it, I'll be right behind you."

We drove up to the bend and saw the tree. It was twice the size of the one that had made us turn around. We decided we'd try our luck moving the other tree and drove back. By the time we got there, several other vehicles were lined up. "Anyone have a chainsaw?" John asked.

"Guy that lives over there went to get one," the man in the car in front of us answered.

And so, we strangers worked to cut up that tree, and another, and another, as we slowly made our way home.

The next morning, as John and I walked up to feed the cattle, we saw trees torn from the ground within yards of his mother's house. We walked into the woods and saw the pattern of uprooted trees -- some of them over 50 feet tall. We envisioned the tornado dancing up and down the sides of the gulley. We stared at the trees in awe of the force of nature and were thankful we had escaped her wrath.

The second storm rose up from the oppressive humidity that clings to the earth during most Missouri summers. The heat had been ghastly for over a week and we had not had rain. That afternoon it clouded up and I considered whether to water the vegetable garden or wait to see if it rained. It blew over, so I decided to wait and see. John got home just after dark and started dinner -- a dinner of summer sausage, cheese, crackers, and fruit, which we would eat by candlelight. The lights began to flicker before dinner was ready and we heard thunder grumbling. I decided to light some candles just in case. Just as I lit the first one, the power went out. I went to the back of the house to make sure the dogs stayed calm. We adopt strays and have twenty-seven dogs, so keeping them calm is no small task. Nothing would keep them calm that night -- they were terrified, and so were we, when the house began to moan and scream. It sounded like the roof was being torn away. I stood in the candlelit hallway and uttered soothing words to our cowering dogs.

What seemed an eternity later the winds died down. John opened the door to the hallway. He told me he'd gone outside and the house had lost some siding. He was going up the road to check on his mom and would be right back. I went around and lit more candles, but John still had not come home. I started to fear the worst and considered going up to help him in case his mother was injured, but I decided against it. He would come get me if he needed me and the dogs were still very nervous. Besides I didn't want to leave the house with candles burning. He finally came home and told me about how he'd had to walk up to her house because there were so many trees down across the road, but that she was fine. She'd slept through the whole thing.

We sat down to eat dinner and drank the chilled white wine greedily. The storm had done nothing to relieve the oppressive heat. After dinner, we stayed up and talked a bit then tried to sleep naked on top of the covers. All the windows were open, but there was no movement in the air. We slept fitfully and in the middle of the night I woke up thirsty. I went to the sink for water and realized that without electricity we had no water. I got ice from the freezer and crunched it as the gravity of our situation sunk in. We were fifteen miles from town with no water and the roads were blocked by trees. I tried to remember what we had to drink. A few bottles of wine, a few cans of soda, yesterday's half pot of coffee. And what about the animals? We have two gallon waterers, but how full were they? Was the pond water drinkable if it was boiled? And how would we boil it? The thought of lighting a fire in this heat was unbearable. When the ice was gone, I lay by the window and tried to go back to sleep, but I was in full-blown panic. I was sure we were going to die and I told John that.

"It'll be ok," he said. "Go to sleep."

I stayed awake by the window. Sometime before dawn, I heard a roar. Not the roar of thunder or wind, but that of an engine. And I saw a light flashing across the trees. I looked out the window and saw a tree pusher moving the trees off the road. Behind it was a line of cars -- people who had been trapped in the woods by the storm. My panic eased. We weren't trapped. At the very least, John would be able to drive to town and buy water.

8

It was a week before power was restored. On the third day, we were finally able to buy a generator. It wouldn't run the water pump or the air conditioner, but we could run a fan, a couple lights, and the computers. We had survived nature's wrath a second time.

As the leaves changed colors and fell away from the trees, the shattered bones of the woods stood stark against the sky. Limbs hung dejectedly and some trees were split in two -- their spirits not quite free. I thought about how many years some of those trees had listened to the sounds of these woods and how many stories they must know. I told John what I was thinking and we agreed that we should publish our own collection of short stories named *Bones of the Woods*.

The third storm arrived in early December. I had just begun to write "The Protectors" that afternoon. The weather report threatened a mix of snow and ice. I encouraged John to close the shop early and come home. It was cold, so he planned to make chili for dinner and I was looking forward to its warmth. By the time he arrived home, the freezing rain had started. As he got the chili going, the lights started to flicker. "I hope we don't lose power," I said.

"We won't," he assured me.

I went back to writing. Fortunately, I was using my laptop because the power did go out. We settled for cold cuts and crackers for dinner instead of the chili we'd craved. John went out to get wood and hurried back in for the tape recorder and camera. "I thought it was someone shooting," he said. "I thought how stupid can someone be to be out poaching in an ice storm. Then I realized I was listening to trees and branches falling."

That night and, in fact, for several days, we listened to trees and branches, already weakened by the summer storms, snap and crash to the ground under the weight of the ice. The next morning, the world was a glistening fairyland. I took picture after picture, including the cover picture and some of the others in this book. It was beautiful, yet harsh. We took turns tending the fire, but we were lucky to have one. Many didn't. We also had the generator and I finished writing "The Protectors" dressed in layers of clothing, sandwiching my words between crunching through the ice to get wood and stoking the fire. Although I didn't write it until a month later, the idea for "The Thaw" rose from the embers of that fire.

And here it is, verging on summer again -- the summer of 2007. So far we've had no violent storms (let's hope it stays that way) and our book of short stories is ready for you -- our readers. It is you who will make us "Immortal".

The Bones of the Forest

By Rachelle Reese

Late July – not sure of the date and can't look at my calendar

I was angry when the power went off at quarter after four. I'm anxious to be finished and rejoin the world I exiled myself from three months ago so I could finish this novel. The novel is close – so close I can taste the closing words on my tongue. Bittersweet, the way I like them.

Amanda flipped through the pages of the red leather-bound journal, looking for a name, a year. She found nothing. She had found the book and two nice ink pens under a floorboard in the crumbling house near the edge of the property her parents had bought last year. Her father

11

had gotten a job in the mines nearby and they were hoping for a fresh start away from the addicted city. That was what her father called all cities. He had been raised in the country and hated the traffic and the rude neighbors honking their horns and then smiling their fake smiles at each other over four-foot fences. Hated the identical houses that stretched endlessly side-by-side with exactly twenty feet between them. Hated the mind-numbing, vitamin water that flowed from every drinking water tap. So when scientists discovered that the tiff rock in the Undiscovered Foothills could be ground and processed to create an anti-anxiety medicine, her father was one of the first to sign up.

Amanda's mother had not been happy. "You know you're a hypocrite, don't you? You know they'll put that medicine you're mining right into the water."

"I'll be mining it, not drinking it," her father had replied. "They'll do what they want with or without me. I plan to build a house with a well."

And so their arguments went. But in the end, her father got the job, they bought ten acres of land, and, five weeks ago, they moved in.

They had lived in the new house just over a month when Amanda discovered the crumbling house. "Why do they call it the Undiscovered Foothills if people lived here before?" Amanda had asked at dinner that night.

"People never lived here, Amanda," her mother had said. "Not in my lifetime."

"They did live here once though. I found a house."

Her mother had become visibly nervous. "Don't go near it. Terrorists might have lived there. There might be bombs, chemicals, and who knows what else." She'd glared at

Amanda's father. "I told you it was a bad idea to move outside of civilization."

Her father had shrugged, "It's probably harmless, Julie. There were lots of people who lived in rural areas before the terrorist attacks. And most of them were just normal people."

"Still."

"Don't worry, Mom," Amanda had learned that it was sometimes easier to just go along with her mother's worries than to argue with her, especially since they'd moved. "I won't go back there. It's too long a walk, anyway."

Of course, Amanda had gone back. There was nothing better to do. She had three more weeks before she could enroll in school. That was the rule when you moved out of the safety net – seven weeks of quarantine. It was the same way going back inside. That's why most people who lived in the cities never left. Who could stand sitting at home and doing nothing for seven weeks?

So Amanda had spent most of last week exploring the house. From what she could tell, a woman had lived there alone. The clothing was mostly rotted away, but she could tell it was old by the style. Pre-terrorist more than likely, maybe even older than that. There were stacks of books, but most of them were too moldy to read. There were dishes stacked in cupboards and piled in an old-style sink. There were even a few old cans of food. Amanda could barely make out the expiration dates, but she was pretty sure they had all expired before she was born.

She had noticed the loose floorboard yesterday and it had bothered her all night. Her imagination ran wild. It could be just a loose floorboard or it could be a passageway to a secret world or a tomb. Or a room full of bombs, her mother's voice interrupted her daydream. Amanda pushed it aside. After all, her father had come from outside the city and he wasn't a terrorist. So first thing in the morning, Amanda had taken the crowbar from her father's toolbox and gone back to the house.

And now she had a book and two very old pens. At first she'd been disappointed, but then she'd realized that the book might help her solve the mystery of who had lived in the crumbling house and what had happened to her.

I'm hoping the power won't be off long, but I can't see a reason it's off at all. There's not a cloud in the sky and the winds are still, unusually still for this time of year. And I'm sure I paid the bill. Well, if it's not on tomorrow I'll drive down to Kyle's Gas and Grocery and use the pay phone there to call. I knew I should have kept that old wire phone. You never know when you'll need one.

Next morning – still no power
And today promises to be ghastly. I didn't sleep much last night. The air was so warm and still I couldn't breathe. It was even hot outside. Tornado weather, they call it. Maybe that's why there's no power. I never realized how dependent I am on electricity. I'm out of practice writing with paper and pen and I can't even get a glass of water because there's no power to run the pump. So here I am drinking yesterday's coffee cold. This would happen two days before I'd planned to make a supply run. Well, off to Kyle's. If nothing else, I can buy some bottled water.

Same day, afternoon
I've spent my whole life writing novels, trying to make them suspenseful, yet realistic. If I'd written about today

14

my editor would have sent it back as too far-fetched. Well, I'm writing it now. And it is reality, not fiction.

I went to Kyle's to call the electric company and buy a few things to tide me over until the power comes back on. When I pulled up, I knew something was wrong right away. Kyle's is never empty. There are always a couple old men out front whiling away the day and at least a person or two at the pumps. Kyle charges more than anyone in town, but he's a good ten miles from any other station, so he gets plenty of business. Got plenty of business. I parked right in front and went inside. There was Kyle, face down next to the cash register in a pool of blood. From the smell, it seemed he'd been dead a day or two, but you never know. As hot as it is, a body would rot pretty fast. And wouldn't you know, the power is out there too. Well, I went to the pay phone. First I tried to call 911. It rang and rang without an answer. Next, I tried the power company. This time I got the after hours recording. I pressed 2 to report a power outage and eventually a person with a heavy Indian accent answered. "I need to report an outage," I said.

"We are aware of the problem, mum. But we cannot contact the office. We think it might be ..."

"What do you mean you can't contact the office? Where are you?"

"Mumbai. India."

"Great. Just great. My power is out in the middle of the United States of America and my call gets answered in Mumbai, India. Where the hell is Mumbai, India?"

"It used to be Bombay, mum."

15

I hung up the phone. Just my luck. I'd have to drive all the way to Park Hills to get answers. And I only had a quarter tank of gas. I took three bottles of water from the warm refrigerator and started to put a ten dollar bill on the counter, then changed my mind. Kyle didn't need the money now and someone would probably just steal it anyway. When whoever he left the store to reopened, I'd settle up then.

I grabbed a couple bags of chips and a candy bar and stepped back outside. Then I noticed the stench. It was bad inside, but it was almost worse outside. And the sound of crows was deafening. I thought about leaving, and probably should have, but I've always been dangerously curious. So I followed the squawking and found the bodies just in time to see a crow tear a piece of flesh from one old man's face and hop to the side to eat it. The other body was unrecognizable, so much flesh had been torn away. But from the clothing, I figured he was probably the other old man who always stood out front. Killing Kyle, I could almost understand. He was a greedy man who watered down his gas and shorted people change. The two old men were harmless characters who'd like nothing better than to tell you the rambling story of their lives. I couldn't imagine someone killing either one of them.

At this point, I was anxious to leave there. I planned to drive to the police station in Park Hills to report the murders and ask them if they knew anything about when the electricity would be turned back on.

I drove back down the curvy roads, past my house, and the other way. I passed no one, which is not unheard of but a little odd. When I got to the highway, it was a different story. It was clogged with cars and trucks – and every single one of them was standing still. Their engines weren't even running. And then I saw the people – hunched over steering wheels, lying at the side of the road, some in pools of blood, others with their faces contorted in unexplained agony. I stared at the carnage, trying to disbelieve it all. It was heatstroke, not real. I took a swig from the water bottle I'd opened when I left Kyle's. As I threw back my head, I heard something smack across my windshield. I jumped, spilling half the bottle of water in my lap. But I didn't even notice that until later because a man, very much alive, was clawing at my windshield. His face was distorted, pressed tight against the glass, his fingers left bloody smears, and he was shouting something I couldn't make out.

I panicked, threw the car into reverse and backed down the country road as fast as I dared. He still clung there, screaming his incomprehensible scream. I slammed on the brakes. The screaming man flew threw the air and hit the ground. I backed down the road until I found a driveway I could turn around in. I thought about going back to see if the man was dead or alive. But something about his screaming mouth terrified me. I decided to stop by Kyle's for more supplies and just go home. I'd take enough to last a week or two.

So that's what I did. Now I just have to wait it out. I'll try to go to town again in a few days. By then maybe the National Guard will have cleaned up the mess.

Amanda's watch warned her it was lunch time. She put the book and the pens carefully back where she had found them and replaced the floorboard. They were safe there for all this time, they'd have to be safe for longer. If her mother found the journal, she'd never hear the end of it.

As she walked through the woods back to her house, her mind raced so fast, she didn't notice the chiggerweed until she came out of it and realized her skin was crawling. Chiggerweed was one of the only things her father had warned her about. "You'll have no immunity to them," he said. "They're bad enough for an old country boy like me, but for a city girl like you they'll be hell." She tried to brush them off, but by the time she got home, she knew that some had bitten into her flesh. Fortunately, her father was at the table when she walked in.

"Dad, I did something stupid."

"You didn't go back to that house, did you?" her mother asked.

Amanda ignored her mother's question. "I wasn't paying attention and I walked through chiggerweed." She held up her ankle, which was just starting to blister.

Her father ran his finger over on of the bumps. "That might be a chigger bite. You'll know soon enough. For now, you'd better go take as hot a bath as you can stand and try to get them off you."

"If it's chiggers, what'll they do to her?" Amanda heard her mother ask as she ran off to the bathroom.

"Itch like a mother-fucker."

"Luke! I hate it when you talk like that."

"What? It's the truth. Have you ever had a chigger bite?"

"Of course not."

"Well I have. And they itch like a mother-fucker."

Amanda hurried off to take the hottest bath she'd ever taken.

***

"Dad, what were the terrorist attacks like?" Amanda was helping her father burn off weeds so they could plant some grass. What she really wanted to do was go back to the house and read more of the journal, but there was no getting out of helping this afternoon.

"I was just a little boy, Amanda. And they didn't strike where I lived."

"Then why did you move to the city?"

"The government put up the nets a few years after the attacks started. They said it was the only safe place to be. My parents believed them, like most people back then. And so they sold their land to the government and moved to the city."

"What happened to the land?"

"Like this, I imagine. Just wasted space until some pharmaceutical company finds a resource on it."

"Do you think they'll strike again?"

"Who?"

"The terrorists."

"They're all long dead, Amanda. The government rounded them all up and injected them with some concoction. Humane execution, they called it."

"What if some escaped?"

"Well, if they did, they must not be interested in terrorism anymore. There hasn't been a terrorist attack in over twenty years."

19

"Do you think there was a terrorist strike here?"

"Here? No, that's doubtful. All the strikes I heard about were in big cities. That's why they blamed us rural folk for the outbreak."

"Outbreak?"

"The terror outbreak. That's why your mother's so paranoid about that old house. The government convinced people that all the terrorists were from rural areas. So you'd be safer inside the net. Believe me, quarantine back then was not the piece of cake it is now. You had to be careful what you said. I know several people who never made it out of quarantine."

"Where are they now?"

"Dead, I imagine. Or in some asylum. I never tried to track them down. Some things you're just better off not knowing."

"What do you mean?"

Amanda's father just shook his head and lit the gasoline on fire. The fire spread fast. It had been a hot, dry summer. "Man the hose, Amanda. Don't let the fire break through!"

Amanda watched for embers and hosed them down. She made sure every little flame was out.

Another hot morning

I sat on the back porch all night and watched the full moon creep across the motionless tree line. It was too hot inside to sleep, so I surrounded myself with citronella candles and braved the mosquitoes. It's been two nights now with almost no sleep and I'm beginning to wonder if the horrific events of yesterday were only a waking nightmare caused by exhaustion and heat. Something that awful cannot be real. So today I will worry only about surviving until the power comes on. I'll drive back down to Kyle's and fill my tank and some gas cans with gas. If the heat continues, I can at least sit in the car with the air conditioning on for a short time.

Early evening

The heat broke this afternoon – at last – with strong winds, lightning and rain. I stood in the rain and felt almost clean for the first time in days. Tonight I'll celebrate by barbecuing the steaks I had in my freezer. I checked them and they were still cool to the touch, so they should be fine. Tonight, for once, I'll sleep.

It's a beautiful night. The world is bathed in pumpkin light. The sun is falling, falling. I will sleep.

Morning

A good night's sleep and I'm convinced that nothing I saw was real. I will drive to Park Hills today and get the power restored.

Days later

It's real. There. I said it. I killed the crazy man and the cars were still there, all backed up on the highway and going nowhere. And it's all too fucking real. Crows and other predators had eaten on most of the corpses, so even if the government did find them, they'd be hell to identify. So what have I been doing? Crying mostly. Crying because there's a pretty good chance that no one will ever read what I'm writing, let alone the novel I hid myself away to finish. But for some reason, I'm still alive. Alone. And when I die, that will be the end.

Early autumn

It's been some time since I wrote. I figured it wasn't worth wasting the ink if there was no one left to read it. But, to hell with that. I'm a writer. It's what I do. And who knows...there might be someone out there, somewhere.

It's amazing what you can hear when you listen to the woods and there are no cars, no airplanes, and no helicopters. For example, I hear a bird whistling, high and strong, and crickets chirping, and frogs singing because it rained today. It probably won't be so bad being the only person left alive. As long as I survive, of course. And if I don't, well there'll be no one around to bury me, so I guess I'll be crow food like all the others.

Anyway, I've decided to try to tell the story of what I think happened. I'm a strange one to tell that story, since I was outside of the world when it happened, but looking back there are some things that should have served as a warning.

First, there were the helicopters. Some nights I'd be up late writing – I miss writing at night – and I'd hear a helicopter flying low. Sometimes it would fly so low, I'd be afraid it might clip the treetops. It was dark, after all. I didn't think anything of it at the time, but looking back now it does seem odd. Why would a helicopter fly low across the forest in the middle of the night? Unless it was doing something illegal. Drugs, maybe? Weapon smuggling? I'm not sure. And what does that have to do with what happened? Maybe nothing. We'll see where the story goes.

It was getting hard for Amanda to read the words. At first she thought maybe the ink was smeared or the page was dirty. But then she looked up from the book and realized the sun was low in the sky. She'd better go. As it was, it would be dark when she got home. Her mother would be hysterical. She placed the book carefully back in its hole and put the floorboards over it.

Then she started home. Her ankles felt like they were on fire, which reminded her to go around the chiggerweed. It was a longer path, but she really didn't want more chiggers. All around her, the world was pumpkin-colored and a bird with a high-pitched squeal sang in the trees as she walked. She guessed the chirping sound might be crickets and made a mental note to ask her father. There were crickets in the city, but nowhere near as deafening as these. As she hurried down the trail, the world changed from pumpkin to rose and then to violet. Luckily, she could see the lights of the house up ahead. She'd really hate to get lost in the woods in the middle of the night. Besides, she could hear thunder rumbling in the distance.

When she walked in the door, her mother was pacing. Up and down the kitchen floor, she walked. "It's all your fault that terrorists kidnapped her!" she yelled at Amanda's father.

"There are no terrorists. Relax," he said. "Calm down. It's just the water. You're not used to it yet."

"You and your water. That's why we're here in the first place, isn't it. Because you had to have your vitamin-free water."

Amanda closed the door. "I'm here, Mom. Relax."

"Where have you been?"

"Just out walking. I lost track of time."

"How can you lose track of time? You have a watch. And you have eyes. Couldn't you see it was getting dark?"

23

"I was listening to the crickets and they put me to sleep."

Her father ran to the door and stuck his head outside. "Those aren't just crickets singing, Amanda. Hear the deeper sounds? And the higher giggling answer? Those are frogs. It's going to rain. Isn't that wonderful? The frogs are telling us it's going to rain. You don't get that inside the safety net. Come, both of you. Listen and smell."

Amanda walked over to her father and he put his arm around her. She took a deep breath. "Smells like a shower, only cleaner."

"That's little droplets of water."

"Water has a smell?"

"Rain has a smell."

Amanda looked over her shoulder and noticed her mother had left the room. "Why is Mom going crazy?"

"I'm not sure, Amanda. I think it's a withdrawal symptom. Remember, for her whole life she's drank water inside the safety net. Now she's drinking pure, fresh well water. No added chemicals. I think her mind is just overwhelmed."

"Will she get better?"

"I hope so. If not, maybe she can find a doctor who will give her pills. But I hope it doesn't come to that. I really want us all to be alive here. Do you feel alive, Amanda?"

"More than ever, Dad."

"Not bored any more?"

"Not bored at all."

"Good." He kissed her forehead and the two of them stood in silence and watched the storm.

After it was over, he asked, "What did you think?"

"Beautiful," she replied. "Beautiful, but frightening at the same time. I was afraid the trees would snap in half."

"They do sometimes. But this storm was mild. They can get much worse. I've seen trees pulled out of the ground, roots and all."

"Is it the lightning that causes the power to go out?"

"What a funny question. There haven't been storm-related power outages since I was a boy. See, these days they run the wires underground. Back then, they ran them above ground so trees could fall on the lines and knock out the power. What have you been reading?"

"Just a book I found."

"You've been to the old house, haven't you?"

"Don't tell Mom."

"Of course not. Is there anything interesting there?"

"All kinds of stuff! Clothes, dishes, books. The person who lived there was a writer."

"How do you know that?"

"I found her journal. That's what I've been reading." Amanda shut up suddenly. She wished she hadn't said anything about the journal. She remembered her father saying 'Some things you're better off not knowing' and wondered if he believed it. If he did, the journal definitely fell into that category.

"What does it say?"

"Oh nothing much. Just stuff about her life."

"Well, maybe when you get done with it, you'll let me read it."

Amanda shrugged, "Sure, Dad." She kissed her father on the cheek and excused herself to go to bed.

Amanda fell asleep easily, but woke in the middle of the night. She could swear she heard a helicopter flying low over the trees. She got out of bed and went to the window, opening it wide. There was no helicopter light, but she could swear she heard the whirring of the blades. And she no longer smelled rainwater. Instead she smelled something that reminded her of vitamins.

I'm not really sure how much time has passed since the power went out. I know it was hot then, I think late July and now the leaves are starting to turn yellow and red. I can almost see them turn. It's amazing the things you notice when you've got nothing much to do. Last night I watched the sunset change my world – because it is _my_ world now – from bright blues and grays to deep amber, then to rose, and then finally to twilight blue. A rainbow in succession. And through it all, black dragonflies darted back and forth, resting briefly on a blade of grass, and then darting off in a different path. It was watching that sunset that made me realize I needed to write again. If only to recapture my world so that someone else knows I existed and that the dragonflies existed and the monarchs and the crows.

The crows are very much still here. One laughs at me every afternoon. I think it's waiting for me to die. But I've made up my mind not to. The main thing is to drink and eat. I've found a spring where I can gather water. I started drinking there some time ago. At first just a little to make sure it didn't make me sick. But now I drink exclusively from the spring. Food is another issue. I've eaten nearly everything from Kyle's. But I can fish. There's a lake nearby and there are poles and lures at Kyle's. There were also some vegetable seeds on a sale rack at the feed store down the road from Kyle's. I've taken some and started lettuce, spinach, and tomatoes in pots. I've never had a green thumb, but perhaps given the necessity, I'll be able to keep them alive.

I've considered learning to hunt too. I'm sure I can find guns and ammunition if I search other houses. I shot a gun once at a target. I needed to know how it felt to shoot a shotgun so that I could write about it correctly. I'm not accurate, but I'm sure I'd get better. That's one thing I definitely don't understand. Most of the people who died were murdered – beat up, strangled, shot. The highway was like a battleground where neither side survived to claim the victory. What made all those people kill each other? I struggle with the idea of killing a squirrel or a wild turkey for sustenance. I can't imagine killing another human being.

On the way home, Amanda played close attention to the leaves of the trees. Very green – that's how she'd describe them. Greener than anything she'd ever seen.

After she got home, she found her father. "When do the leaves turn colors?"

"Another month or so. Why?"

"The writer told about it in her journal. I wanted to see it."

"It's beautiful, Amanda. You'll love it. The air has a different smell then, too?"

"Like vitamins?"

"No. Why would it smell like vitamins?"

"Last night something woke me up and when I went to the window, I smelled vitamins."

"It must still be that water working its way out of your system. You still have another week of quarantine, you know. You're body's still flushing out the poison."

"Dad, why do they call it vitamins and you call it poison?"

"I just don't think people need it, sweetheart. That's all."

"How's Mom tonight?"

"Better. I think the withdrawal might be ending."

"I hope so."

"Me too, Amanda. Me too."

***

A cool day

It's cool this morning. Cool enough for me to put on sweats and a sweatshirt instead of the shorts and t-shirts that have been my uniform since I exiled myself last May. Also cool enough to remind me that winter does come eventually to this part of the world. So today I took the axe out of the shed to start cutting fallen trees into firewood. The axe was left here by the previous owner. They also left a splitting hammer. Chopping wood is something I've done before. As a young girl, I helped my father cut wood. But it's not something I thought I'd ever do again. Usually I purchase a rank or two of wood for cozy fires on the evenings I need extra comfort. Fire has always been more an emotional thing for me than a physical necessity. This winter, fire will keep me alive.

As I held the axe in my hand, I thought again about the people who'd murdered and been murdered. I wondered what it would feel like to split a skull with an axe, as one woman's had been at a farmhouse I visited looking for eggs. Her head was split in two and a man lay nearby her, a bullet through his nasal cavity. I guess he wanted to be sure he didn't linger. Of course, I did murder in the mad heat of summer. I threw the crazy man from my windshield. But I consider that self defense. At least that's how I think about it now. If it had been murder, I would have made sure he was dead by backing over him or something. That's not what I did. I just removed him from my windshield.

Judge, jury, defendant, and prosecutor. Some days I feel like I have split in to all four. It's not too different from writing a novel – you are your characters to some extent. The difference here is that each one is really me. There is no characterization or plot development. It is just me, playing out my different roles. Splitting hairs.

Splitting wood. I held the block against the top of the log and brought it down hard. The log splintered and fell into four pieces. Kindling. Essential when starting a fire without fire starters. Speaking of fire starters. I think I saw a few at Kyle's – leftover from last winter most likely. But a few are better than nothing. Especially on days when I have to use wet wood. And matches. I'll need to pick up matches next time I'm there.

The shed is still there; Amanda remembered seeing it. She wondered if the axe and splitting hammer were still there. She'd been so busy exploring the house and reading the journal that she hadn't even looked in the shed.

She put the book back in its spot and replaced the floorboard. Then she walked to the shed. Like the house, it was crumbling and the paint had peeled off almost completely. She tried the door and it opened. Didn't people lock anything in those days, she wondered. She stepped inside. It was mustier than the house and dark. She propped the door open to get as much light as she could. No good. She would have to come back with a light stick.

As she left, she tried to imagine where the woodpile might have been. Close to the house, probably. At least that's where she'd put it. The safety net didn't keep the cities from getting cold. Amanda had shivered on many a cold morning when she'd had to walk to the subway station to take the subway to school. She wondered how warm a fire could keep you. She'd never seen a fire before. They were outlawed in the safety net. And even accidental fires were rare. Guns were outlawed too, even outside the safety net. Amanda wondered if there was a gun in the house. If there was, should she tell anyone?

Walking through the tall grass on the way back to the house, Amanda stubbed her toe on something. She looked down and saw a rotted wooden stick with a large metal mallet. It looked like a hammer, but much larger. She bent down to take a closer look and noticed slender white sticks arranged almost in the shape of a hand. Then she realized she wasn't looking at sticks. She was looking at the bones of a hand. She carefully moved the grass around and found two arms, two legs, rib bones, and even a skull. She felt a shiver run down her spine. She was sure she was looking at the woman who wrote the journal. Amanda's scream joined the noises of the forest and she started to run. She was halfway home before she stopped running. "I'm being stupid," she told herself. "The woman had been dead for years. She probably starved to death that winter or maybe even froze." She tried to calm herself as she walked toward the house. "Otherwise Mom will ask a million questions." Deep breaths. Concentrate on something different, like that butterfly over there. Or that one. There are a lot of butterflies today. Just keep walking calmly. Back to the house. So you touched a dead person's bone. It's not like it's the first time. Remember anatomy class? You touched lots of bones there. It's no different."

"He-he-he-he-he-haw," something laughed.

Amanda looked into the forest, "Who's there?"

A crow swooped down from one of the trees and pecked at something on the ground. Amanda turned her head away, refusing to look.

***

Amanda didn't tell anyone about the skeleton, even her father. But she didn't go back to the house for a long time after, either. Her seven weeks of quarantine ended, along with her father's and mother's. On the evening before the interview, her father asked her to walk with him in the woods.

"Are you nervous about tomorrow, Amanda?"

"A little. What will they do?"

"I don't know exactly. This is my first interview since my family moved to the safety net when I was twelve."

"What did they do then?"

"They asked me questions about how I liked the city, what I missed most about the country, and my intentions. It went easier for me than for my brother."

"Uncle Tony?"

"Yes. He was labeled as a potential terrorist."

"Why?"

"He told them the truth. He was older than me and he'd seen more. He had suspicions that innocent people were being imprisoned as terrorists. And back then, Tony didn't know how to keep quiet."

"What did they do?"

"Sent him away to an asylum for awhile to be 'educated'. Brainwashed is more like it if you ask me. And once a year he has to be interviewed, even now."

The two sat together for a few moments, listening to the frogs. Finally, Amanda spoke up, "You don't think they'll send Mom away, do you?"

"I don't know, Amanda. I'm hoping they'll just give her some medicine to see if that helps. Or maybe she'll have a good day tomorrow."

"And how about you?"

"I know what to say to them. Don't you worry about your Dad."

"And me?"

"I wouldn't tell them about the house if I were you. Or what I've told you about the water and the terrorists. Just stick to stuff a normal sixteen year old would care about."

Amanda rolled her eyes back and stuck out her tongue. "Are you saying I'm not normal?"

Her father laughed and ran his fingers through her reddish-brown hair. It had gotten long since they'd lived outside the city. "Would any daughter of mine be just normal?"

Amanda laughed and kissed her father on the cheek, "I love you Dad."

The two of them sat for a long time, watching the fireflies and listening to song of the forest.

***

"How do you like being outside the safety net?" the portly man in the dark suit asked.

"I like it. There are a lot of new things to see."

"Like what?" asked woman in the green one-piece pantsuit.

"Trees, frogs, fireflies, birds. Mostly just stuff in the woods. I haven't spent any time in town yet."

"What are your intentions?" the man asked.

"I'm looking forward to starting school and meeting new friends."

"Do you miss your friends?" asked the woman.

"Sometimes. Especially when I'm bored."

"In your opinion, how are your parents adjusting?" the woman leaned toward her confidentially.

"My Dad loves it. He's excited about starting his new job. Plus he likes to teach me things."

"Teach you things? What sorts of things?" the man scowled.

"Just stuff about nature – you know, like frogs and crickets and chiggers. He grew up in the country."

"That's right. I see that here," the woman consulted a thick folder with her father's name printed in the corner.

"By the way, you didn't ask me if there's anything I hate. Chiggers would be what I hate." Amanda tried to change the subject from her mother.

"Chiggers?" the man leaned closer. "What's a chigger?"

"Awful little red bugs. My Dad says they liquefy the skin. Look, this is what chigger bites looks like," Amanda put her foot up on the coffee table and rolled down her sock.

The man leaned closer to take a look.

"Don't get too close," Amanda warned. "If the chiggers haven't dropped off yet, they'll get on you. And believe me, you don't want that. You would have no immunity to them at all."

Amanda rolled up her sock and put her foot back on the ground. The woman reached for a can of disinfectant and sprayed down the coffee table. She looked up at Amanda, "You can go."

The man had taken out his magnifying glass and was examining the coffee table's surface. "Make a note to look up chiggers when we get back to the city," he said. "It might be a code name for chemical weapons. Did you see the bumps on her ankle?"

"Don't be paranoid, Karl," the woman said. "They probably were just bug bites. Remember, she hasn't had vitamins in seven weeks. Her system is probably breaking down."

Amanda closed the door behind her and part of her hoped she had left a chigger or two behind. Well, at least she'd avoided talking about her mother.

Amanda enrolled for school the next day. She had only fifteen students in her graduating class – a definite change from the 350 in her city school. Like her, they had all recently moved from the city because a parent had gotten a job for the pharmaceutical company.

Unlike her, the rest of them lived in the small new town. The town had a single school for all grades, a grocery store, a pharmacy, two sit-down restaurants, a deli, a hamburger place, and a dozen or so shops. Most of the shops were owned by spouses of people who worked for the pharmaceutical company.

On the first day of school, no one said a word to her. In fact, no one said much of anything, except when the teacher called on them. Amanda figured they had just gotten out of quarantine like her and were shy. She sat down next to one of the other girls at lunch, "I'm Amanda."

"Kylie."

"Have you lived here long?"

"Three months tomorrow. How about you?"

"I just got through quarantine yesterday."

"Do you miss the city?"

"Not so much. How about you?"

"I hate it here. And I'm going to say so on my next interview. Do you think they'll send me back?"

"You have to go through another interview?"

"Don't you?"

"No. At least I don't think so." Amanda thought back on what they'd said to her yesterday. She knew her mother had to go back in a month to see how the pills they'd prescribed were working. But as far as she knew, she was home free.

"All the kids I talk to have to go twice a year. Just to make sure the dosage is right on the vitamins. You know, they don't put vitamins in the water out here. It means we could die. I almost did."

"You almost died?"

"Sure," Kylie lowered her voice. "About three weeks after we moved out here, I started hearing voices."

"What did they say?"

"They told me I was worthless and that I should just get it over with."

"What do you mean?"

"You know, off myself."

"Good thing you didn't," Amanda was dumbfounded. She had heard of suicide happening in the past – Marilyn Monroe, Ernest Hemingway, some of the terrorists in prison. But she'd never known anyone who actually considered it.

Kylie shrugged, "I guess. Anyway, I told my mother what I was feeling. She's a pharmacist, so she knew right away what was wrong. She called one of her friends in the city and they hooked me up with some vitamin replacement pills to last until my first interview. Now I get them legitimately, of course. Just like everyone else."

"What does everyone do for fun around here?"

"Fun?" Kylie looked confused for a minute. "Oh, there's a movie theater. And they say they're going to put in a skating rink, but it might not be ready this winter. Some of the kids hang out at The Grill on the Hill. Darryl's Mom

36

owns it, so Darryl and his friends get a discount." Kylie pointed to a good-looking blonde boy sitting with each arm around a different girl.

"Which one's his girlfriend?" Amanda asked.

"Neither. They both just hang out with him for the discounted food. No one really likes Darryl. His father's one of the top scientists at the company and Darryl lets it go to his head."

"Thanks for the warning."

"You would have figured it out yourself sooner or later."

Just then a bell sounded. "Guess it's time to go back to class," Amanda said.

"Yeah. Another exciting afternoon of Math, History, and Physical Education." Kylie stood up and started back to the classroom. Amanda walked beside her.

***

The things Kylie told her bothered Amanda the rest of the afternoon. Why were all the other kids given vitamins? Why wasn't she? What made Kylie want to kill herself?

At dinner, Amanda watched her mother and father closely. Her mother seemed a little better now. More a worry wart like she'd been before they moved. Less anxious. Her father seemed a little agitated. "How was work, Dad?"

"Pretty much like I expected. Not enough workers and those I have are mindless drones who can't think for themselves. How was school?"

Amanda smiled, "About the same."

Her father looked up from his dinner and nodded. "Take a walk after dinner?"

"I'd love to. I could use some fresh air."

After dinner they walked out through the trees and sat on a rock in a clearing. The air was cool, even a bit nippy.

"Look there," her father said. "Fruit bats."

Amanda watched the small brown creatures swoop down briefly, then fly back up. There must have been a hundred of them, flying together like a huge kite being controlled by an experienced kite flyer, yet each one moving singularly within the mass. "What are they doing?"

"Feeding. They eat insects."

"Are they dangerous?" Amanda had seen enough vampire movies to know that bats fed on human blood.

"Only if you're an insect. They only bite a human if they feel threatened. But watch them. Aren't they beautiful?"

"Mmmhmm," Amanda agreed half-heartedly. She was still not sure she liked being so close to that many bats.

"See this rock here?" her father picked up a small rock and held his light stick to it. "This beautiful rock is what we're mining. Look at the crystal formations."

"It's a geode," Amanda had seen geodes in science class and at the science museum.

"It's not, but it's similar. The amazing thing about rocks is that each one is different. Pick up every single rock here and you'll never find two that are identical."

"Like people," Amanda said.

"Like people should be," her father put the tiff rock down on the slate rock they sat on and ground against it with a metal mallet. Amanda watched part of the rock turn to powder. "After we harvest the tiff rocks, we grind them up like this – even finer. All those beautiful, unique formations ground to identical molecules of dust. And why do we do it?"

"To make medicine for people like Mom?"

"To make something that numbs people's minds. Here, taste." Her father licked his finger and put it in the powder, then placed the powder on his tongue. Amanda did the same.

"Tastes bitter, but it makes my tongue feel funny."

"When they mix it up with other things to make a medicine, that's what it does to your mind."

"Why would people want to feel like that?"

"It's not a choice, Amanda. It's prescribed."

"You mean like the kids at school." Amanda picked up a piece of tiff and examined its crystals.

"What do you mean?"

"They just sit there. Quiet. One girl, Kylie, said they all take pills. She said it was to replace the vitamins they're missing in the water. That without the pills, they'd die."

"You don't take pills. I don't take pills."

"I know. But why didn't they make us take the pills?"

Her father sat there mulling things over, examining a piece of tiff as if it held the answers. Finally he said, "I don't know Amanda. I guess we should just feel lucky."

"We don't have to have another interview do we?"

"We might," her father put the piece of tiff down and stood up. "But we'll get through it. We know how to answer their questions."

Amanda stood up and took her father's hand. "Dad, don't get upset, but I might have said something I shouldn't have."

"What did you say?"

"I told them about the chiggers and showed them my bites."

"What did they say?"

"The man said he wanted to make sure to look them up when they got back to the city. He was worried 'chiggers' might be a code word for terrorists."

Her father's laugh roared out through the woods so loud it startled an owl. The bats scattered. "You know, Amanda. He's not too far from wrong."

The first frost

My arms are hard and strong. My legs are riddled with oozing welts left behind by ticks and chiggers, which I douse daily with hydrogen peroxide. But my diligence paid off. Today, I awoke to frost glittering in the sunlight, blinding in its post dawn assault. I ducked quickly from my blanket to my sweat pants and pulled a sweater over my sweatshirt. Brrrr. I decided I'd better bring some wood inside. But first a fire. I stacked logs in the fireplace, trying to remember what they'd told us in Girl Scouts. Of course, that was a campfire. But a fire in a fireplace can't be much different. Next I added kindling sticks between the logs and crumpled up some newspapers I'd barely skimmed when they were delivered. I struck the match and lit the paper on fire. I held my hands close to the flames. I would need to steal some gloves from somewhere. I hadn't moved in prepared for winter.

Amanda read the words greedily; sorry she'd stayed away for so long. After all, they were only bones. It's not like they could rise up and strike her. Besides, the woman had wanted someone to read her story. She had said so herself.

The paper burned, but the kindling never caught. I would need some other way to get this started. I remembered reading of arsonists who set a fire using rags soaked in gas. I went to my rag bin and pulled out a t-shirt that had been worn away to threads. I ripped it in three pieces, then braided them together, tying each end with a piece of thread. Then I lowered the small rope into the gas can. It soaked up the gasoline quickly. I put the rag in a pan and carried it to the fireplace. Careful not to drip gasoline on the ground, I put it in the fireplace and lit both ends. Like a candle's wick, it came to life. Soon the kindling started burning too. And finally, the logs turned glowing red. I will need to keep the fire burning as long as I can. I don't know how long the gas at Kyle's will hold out.

I heated a can of chili on the fire. It was the first hot meal I'd had since I ran out of charcoal and it was satisfying to feel the warm food fill my mouth and warm me all the way down to my stomach. I can't help thinking about the chickens at the farmhouse about a mile away – now gone free range with no one there to look after them. I wonder whether I could catch one and wring its neck. I have noodles and some canned vegetables. A pot of chicken soup would be delicious. Maybe tomorrow. Today I'll go to Kyle's and see if there are gloves, a coat, and maybe a hat and scarf.

The Farmhouse

Kyle's had no winter clothing, so I drove to the farmhouse. The bodies have mostly decomposed, leaving only bones now. It feels less like I'm stealing from hard-working people. Besides, they won't need winter clothing where they are – wherever that is.

In the bedroom, I found a crib and inside the crib, the skeleton of a small child, draped in blue one-piece pajamas, decorated with embroidered puppies. From the size of the pajamas, I guess the bones belonged to a toddler. The child's skull had been fractured in multiple places. Once again I was amazed at the brutality of man. What could have driven someone to do that to a child? What monster drove the people here to madness?

I went through the closets and the drawers, and found what I needed. I took two pairs of gloves, a scarf, and a winter coat. I decided to take the sweaters and blankets too. It's better to have too much than not enough, I reasoned. I also found some matches, a first aid kit, and some homemade preserves. I loaded it all into my car. One of the free-range chickens pecked around at my feet. I found some stale crackers in the cabinet and threw it to the chickens. I might as well make friends with them. It'll make them easier to catch when the time comes. I imagined my hands circling one of their necks and tossed out a few more crumbs. No. I'm not hungry enough for that yet. I'll stick with canned goods for now.

Amanda's watch rang to warn her it was time to go home. She was going to town with her parents to have dinner and watch a movie. It was a celebration of being done with quarantine. When Amanda got home, her mother was humming happily in the kitchen. She was wearing a soft blue dress, high heels, and her gold chain. Her father was wearing a button-down shirt and slacks. "Better hurry and get dressed," her mother chimed. "Reservations are in an hour."

"Where are we going for dinner?" Amanda asked. She figured either The Grill on the Hill or maybe the Italian restaurant.

"Sebastian's," her mother sang. "Isn't that wonderful?"

"Sure," Amanda hurried to find something she could wear to the finest restaurant in town. She wondered what made her father decide to splurge on Sebastian's. She finally settled on a pair of dark green velvet slacks with a gold scoop necked blouse. She'd bought them for a dinner date before she'd left the city. The guy had been a boring "drone," as her father called them. But that didn't make the outfit any less attractive. Amanda caught a look at herself in the mirror as she left the room. She had to admit she liked her new look. Her hair had grown past her shoulders and her cheeks were flushed with color. She smiled and rushed to meet her parents.

Both her parents seemed to be in an unusually good mood as they drove to the restaurant. Amanda tried to convince herself that it was just because it was their first weekend since quarantine ended. When they got to the restaurant, her father held the door for her mother to step out of the car. He draped his arm gently around her waist, as if they were newlyweds. Amanda followed the two inside.

Their table was waiting and Amanda was surprised that a small town could support such a plush restaurant. The seats were heavily padded in garnet, emerald, and sapphire velvet. The menu was six pages long, with so many elegant, delicious sounding choices that Amanda had trouble deciding. She finally settled on a roasted game hen stuffed with herbed rice. Her father ordered prime rib and her mother ordered filet mignon. For appetizer, her father ordered sautéed frogs legs. Her mother wrinkled her nose and he said, "Have you tried them?"

"No, of course not."

"Then you don't know you won't like them."

"What do they taste like?" Amanda asked.

"A little like chicken, and a little like fish. You'll just have to try them and see."

The waitress brought a basket of fresh rolls and placed it on the table. Then she filled their glasses with water. Amanda looked around. The restaurant was crowded. Most tables held a single couple, a few held two couples, and a few others held a couple and a child.

One table caught her eye. Kylie sat with her parents, staring down at her salad, her face downcast as it had been when school had ended the day before. Her father seemed to be lecturing her about something.

"Your mother and I have a surprise," her own father said. Amanda looked her parents, smiling at her across the table.

"I went to the doctor today to get my prescription," her mother began. "Because I'd been off my medication for almost two months, they did a routine urinalysis."

"What your mother is saying is…"

"Let me tell it my way," her mother stood up and put one hand on her belly. "I'm pregnant, Amanda. You're going to have a baby brother or sister."

Amanda was astonished. Family size was limited to one child by law. The goal was to reduce the population in the cities by half by the end of the century. In the years that followed the terrorist strikes, couples had been anxious to replace those who had been lost. There had also been a renewed sense of security after the safety net was built. The government had let things take their course for fifteen years. But after everyone moved from the country into the safety net, they realized that there was just no room. At first they required a permit for a couple to have more than one child. Then later, they restricted family size through mandatory medication. "But I thought," Amanda started to speak, but was interrupted by her father.

"The law only applies to the cities, Amanda. Here in the country we can have a larger family if we want." Her father was clearly excited. "And the best thing of all is that the doctor thinks your mother can be kept off the medication and deliver a baby who has not been subjected to the vitamins."

Amanda glanced back over at Kylie's table. They had brought the food and her father had stopped lecturing and was intent on his lobster. "I thought the interviewer mandated medication for Mom."

"In light of her present condition, she can request another interview."

"Honey, you'll know soon enough, but pregnancy causes wide emotional swings in some women." Her mother broke open a roll and slathered it with butter and honey. "It also causes an increased appetite. I'm famished."

"Damn it!" Amanda heard a shout from Kylie's table. She glanced over and saw Kylie's father throw the shattered lobster claw down on his plate. "What do you mean you want another one? Don't we have enough trouble

45

with her?" Amanda saw Kylie staring down at her plate, trying to ignore her father's outburst. She felt bad for Kylie. The whole restaurant was staring at her father.

"Control group," someone at a nearby table whispered. "They're giving him placebo."

"How do you know?" the person's companion whispered back.

"Can't you tell by how he's acting? Probably giving the girl placebo too."

"We'll talk about this at home," Kylie's father picked up another claw and cracked it open with too much force, shattering it in small pieces. He savagely ripped the fragments of claw away from the flesh and sucked. The slurping echoed throughout the quiet room. Kylie stood up from the table and walked out. "Where are you going?" her father said loudly.

"To the bathroom."

Amanda noticed that Kylie had her steak knife in one hand and her purse in the other, "Excuse me."

"Where are you going, honey?" her mother asked sweetly.

"To the bathroom."

"Aren't you happy about the baby?"

"Of course, Mom," Amanda didn't know if she was telling the truth or not. "I just have to go."

Amanda rushed to the bathroom and found her new friend sitting on the floor drawing slashes across her arm with the steak knife. "What are you doing?"

"Trying to make them shut up."

"Who, your parents?"

"Them. The voices. Sometimes pain makes them go away," she slashed an X across her forearm.

"I thought you said you didn't hear them anymore."

"I never said that," Kylie looked up at Amanda. Her eyes were wide and reddened. "I hear them and I always will unless I can get them to send me back to the city. Especially now."

"Why now?"

"She's pregnant. Three months. She was going to tell him tonight. I told her not to do it in public, but she thought he'd be happy." Kylie dug into her arm again. "She thought he'd be HAPPY!"

What monster drove the people here to madness? Amanda heard a woman's voice. The same voice she heard in her head each time she read from the journal. She knew the voice was the woman's, the writer's. "Give me the knife, Kylie."

"No," Kylie held the knife close to her body.

"It makes me nervous, Kylie. Please." She moved cautiously toward the girl, "I want to be your friend."

Kylie looked up slowly. "Really?"

"Of course. Why do you think I talked to you at school?"

Kylie put the knife in front of her on the floor. "I'd like that. I had friends in the city, but no one likes me here."

"Besides, we have something in common."

"What?"

"My mother's pregnant too. I found out tonight."

She saw Kylie relax a little. "How is your father taking it?"

"He's ecstatic."

Kylie looked up slowly. "Really?"

"Yeah. It's my mom I'm worried about. She's really happy about the baby, but she's going to go off the pills. And she had a really bad withdrawal when we moved here. Not as bad as yours, but it was pretty bad."

"Why is she going off the pills?"

Amanda realized she'd probably said too much. "I'm not sure. She just is. Maybe they're not good for the fetus."

"My mom's a pharmacist; she would know."

"Maybe she's not taking the pills either."

Kylie looked confused for a moment, "You know, she didn't say. And now you mention it, she has been acting nervous. I just figured it was something to do with being pregnant."

"It could be. Maybe she's nervous about getting your father to accept it."

"He'll never accept it. Not now."

"Has he always been angry like that?"

"No. Just since right after the quarantine interview. First he got really cold to me. I figured it was because he was disappointed in me because I couldn't make it through quarantine and I'd cry every night that I wanted to go back to the city. A few weeks later he started getting angry at everything. It's like nothing makes him happy. He even slapped my mother a few days ago."

"Are you afraid he'll hurt you?"

"Sometimes," Kylie cast her eyes downward and Amanda realized she was looking at the knife.

"The voice is his, isn't it?"

Kylie nodded, "One of them. I don't recognize the other one."

"Is your mother frightened?"

"I don't know. I haven't asked her."

Amanda took her new friend's hand, "I think you should talk to her about it. About everything."

Kylie squeezed Amanda's hand, "Thanks for listening."

The two of them walked hand in hand out into the restaurant, then went to their separate tables.

***

That night Amanda dreamed of a baby, clawing at the bars of a crib to get out. The baby looked on as a shadowy man swung an axe over the mother's head and brought it down. The baby started to cry. The man swung around, dropping the axe. He grabbed the baby from the crib, picking it up by the head with a huge lobster cracker. "Damn it!" the man shouted and split the baby's head in pieces. Then he lifted a piece to his mouth and sucked it dry. Each slurp echoed in the empty nursery.

***

The next morning, Amanda hurried to the crumbling house right after breakfast. She had to know how the story ended.

Fresh spinach

I plucked leaves from the spinach plants today. It's the first fresh vegetables I've had in a long long time. I tasted each leaf, bitter and sweet mixed together into the perfect ending.

I am hopeful tonight, not just because of the spinach, but because my solitude might be coming to an end. I heard a helicopter whirring overhead last night. Just like they did before the power went out. And when I went to Kyle's for some bacon bits and Chex Mix for my first freshly-grown salad, I saw tire tracks that were not mine.

I don't know if they'll find me here, but perhaps they'll clear the road and I'll drive back to civilization on my own. I'll give them a few days to clean up and then I'll check.

In the meantime, the fire roars hot and tiny green tomatoes hang from my tomato plants. If it takes a month or two months, at least I'll eat well while I wait.

That was it. No more entries. But if she was rescued, who did the skeleton belong to? Amanda rushed outside to where she'd seen the bones. She saw women's size 7 shoes lying near the feet. One hand was still encased in a glove, mostly eaten away by weather. Amanda examined the skull. A single bullet was lodged just above the left temple. She wriggled it and it broke free. She squinted at the bullet in the sunlight and read the letters USG4 2014.

"He-he-he-he-he-haw," the familiar laugh rang from the trees nearby. Amanda looked up and saw a crow.

Amanda folded the book under her arm and headed home.

The Hangman's Tree

By Rachelle Reese
Inspired by John E. Miller

Press the knife against the ridge of wrist where tanned muscle gives way to the soft white flesh around the veins. Clean and sharp. Clean like Tom had looked -- clean and shaved and polished against the blue satin lining. Steady now, steady. Fucking this up will leave a scar. Explain that to Nikki. Nikki'll be pissed enough as it is. At least she's not knocked up. That would be worse -- leave behind a genetic consequence for all the pain and pleasure. What was that billboard by the school? A sad-eyed baby and big teary letters. *Who's your daddy? Paternity tests free of charge for Medicare mothers.* At least Nikki never had to worry about that. There wouldn't have been any doubt. If there's one thing Nikki is, it's faithful. Faithful to the end. Don't think about her now. Concentrate on what you have to do. Draw a straight thin line and don't flinch. Just like in

Biology class when you cut open that frog. "You could be a surgeon with those hands," Mrs. Blakely had said. Remember that now and cut straight. There. Just enough pressure to make it bleed. Steady hands, steady heart. If your heart was so steady, why didn't you pick up the phone? One simple call and you were too wrapped up in whether or not Nikki was knocked up to give a damn and pick up the phone. "Tony? You there, Tony?" Tom's voice had called through the answering machine. "Pick up the phone, little brother. I need to talk to you. Pick up the phone, little brother." Over and over the phone rang and those words called out. Again and again while you slept. And those words rang in your ears for the next three days until you saw him, clean and shaved and polished, against the blue satin lining. Rough and jagged was how he'd looked the last time you saw him alive. Rough and jagged like he hadn't slept in week. In a month. "Pick up the phone, little brother." But you couldn't do it. Not even to say hello, sorry not tonight, but we'll get together soon. You couldn't even speak to him long enough to tell him to hang on, to give him something to hang on for.

"Don't let go, Tom!" you'd spoken those words once when you were kids. Tom had fallen from a tree, his head opening up on the pavement; yellow, orange, and brown leaves swimming in bright red. *"Hang on, Tom,"* you'd said. *"I'll go get Mom. I'll get help."* And you ran and ran until you found someone to help. Hang on Tom. You held his hand in the ambulance and even while they stitched him back together. *"Frankenhead,"* you called him and you both laughed. He laughed until his head hurt and he had to lie down. For days you worried that his head would break open and the blood would come pouring out. What were you? Four? Five? And after his head had healed, the two of you would hang upside down from the willow tree and sing *Two hangmen hanging from a tree.* "That's why they call it

a weeping willow," Tom had said and you believed him. You never even tried to find out if it was true. Upside down you'd hang, the blood rushing to your heads and making you dizzy. Tom would somersault over the branch and call for you to do the same. But you couldn't do it, could you? You just hung there and waited for Tom to lift you off the branch and put you on your feet. "You know what you are, Tony? A coward," Tom had laughed.

I'm not a coward today, big brother. Today I'm going to make you proud. Today I'm brave. Brave enough to make the sink turn red. Two hangmen hanging from a tree. That's what we were and what we are. What a gas. I never knew what that meant. But you knew, Tom. You knew even then. Oh god this hurts. Be brave, Tony. Brave and steady. Just let the blood rush out. Two hangmen hanging from a tree. You killed you and I killed me. No one's braver than you and me. No one's deader than you and me.

Tony looked up from the sink and saw a shadow over his shoulder. A man in a dark suit and a dark felt hat stood in the doorway. He didn't speak and didn't move. Tony looked down at the blood pooling against the white porcelain sink. Nikki would have to clean it up -- that's the worst thing about it. Damn my poor planning. Now Nikki would have to clean it up. Tony saw his reflection one last time as his knees collapsed. The bathroom tile felt cold against his cheek - cold and clean and polished.

***

"You know what we'll be tomorrow, Sid? Two hangmen hanging from a hangman's tree. That's what we'll be."

"Quiet, Bill. I need to make my peace with God."

"You've got to appreciate the irony of it though, Sid. Even you should appreciate the irony."

"Bill, let me pray. You should too. The hangman's hereafter is not as black and white as most other folks'."

"Whatever they say, I never hanged a man without due process. Never, not once."

"Bill, let me pray."

"Yessir, we'll hang from a hangman's tree without a hangman around to hang us."

The next morning at dawn, we walked up the hill. The hangman's tree was a black silhouette against the reddening sky. I thought the sky looked angry, but didn't say anything to Sid. He seemed distressed enough and couldn't see the irony in anything. He'd spent all night muttering to his god and he looked like hell. I'd spent all night trying to tune him out by listening to the chorus of frogs and crickets outside my window. From the sounds of things, fall was near. I listened to the frogs argue back and forth and considered the situation from all angles. Ironic. That's the only way to describe it. Ironic and just dead wrong.

The first-time hangman walked behind us and slapped a rope against our legs, "Hurry it up," he said.

One thing I knew was that if it was up to me to decide the fate of the man who pulled the rope today; I would make sure he burned in hell. I sure hope he knew what he was doing. Hanging is an art. Being hanged wrong would be the worst injustice yet. Not to mention, it would be painful. I grimaced as he missed my head the first time he tried to slip on the noose. Would I have to give instructions for my own death? I felt the rope tighten around my neck. Now one swift jerk, I thought to myself. One swift jerk and I'll be swinging from the tree. He pulled the rope slowly and I felt my feet rise off the ground. The rope cut into my neck. This would be worse than I thought. "Jerk hard," I cried. "Jerk hard and fast. You have to break my neck for it to work."

"Shut up," he said. "I'll do it my own way."

I felt the pressure around my neck ease up. My feet nearly touched the ground. "I'm not dead yet, foo..." then crack, black, and nothing. No rope, no pain, nothing. The spine was snapped. Okay, not bad for a rookie. I could have done without the opening rope burn, but at least he cracked the spine. I wondered if Sid was as lucky.

"Heaven or hell?" a voice behind me asked. "Won't be so easy to decide with you. I guess I'll have to flip a coin. You wouldn't have one, would you?" The voice stepped into the circle of light in front of me. It belonged to a woman with long red braids, coiled into a net at the nape of her neck. She wore a velvet and satin dress, like those you think of queens wearing back before the west was won. It was black with purple sleeves.

"I thought angels wore white," I said.

"I'm not an angel," she replied. "That's an angel." I looked just in time to see Sid engulfed in brilliant white flames, then disappear. The flames left behind a momentary void like the darkness in the room when you've looked too long at the sun.

"Then what are you?"

"I'm your destiny."

I felt my lips curl to match her smile. It was a familiar position for them. The hangman's smile, I'd called it often enough. This woman with the long red braids was a professional hangman.

"Executioner," she said. "I prefer being called an executioner. But in the afterlife, my job is more that of judge. And in you, I've met my match. So I can either flip a coin, or..."

"Or?" my eyebrow rose to match the expression on her face.

"Or you can take my place," she twirled a piece of hair that had escaped a braid. "I'm ready to rest now. I've sent kings and queens, peasants and thieves to their just reward. And never, in all that time, have I found someone as truly neutral as you. You'll make a fine replacement."

"Do I have a choice?"

"Not really. You see, if I toss a coin, I admit there's a greater power than mine. It's not in my character to admit that. Besides, as I said, I'm tired. I'm ready for my reward." Her hands were cool as they touched my head, cool enough to penetrate my scalp, my mind, my blood. Cool as mine are now, and as yours will be after you decide. Feel.

Tony felt a coolness on his forehead and opened his eyes. He saw flesh drawn back against bone. Stern and grey, made greyer by the black collar and thin yellow rope time.

"Yes, you're coming around," Bill said. "But you've lost a lot of blood. Lay still and listen to my story. You'll want to hear this part, I'm sure."

"Who are you?"

"My name is Bill. Just leave it at that for now. By the time my story's finished, you'll know more than you want to. Now, where was I? Yes, I remember. The woman with the long red braids had placed her hand on my forehead. She was filling me with her cold, harsh logic. I felt more reasonable than I'd ever felt before; more able to cast

56

judgment and determine right from wrong. The transformation had occurred. My executioner and my salvation smiled one last time and disappeared. An angel stood before me in flowing white robes, a glowing red jewel in his raised up hand. I watched as he ascended to the heavens, colors streaming down from him. I thought I knew the origin of rainbows in that instant -- the soul of a hangman being carried to heaven.

They say when a person dies, there are angels waiting in the wings. That's true when there's no choice to be made. If there's a choice to be made, it's me who waits. It's me who has to judge. Live or die? Heaven or hell?

I tell you, I've had to make some difficult decisions. Take the man who hanged me. It turns out that he and his cohorts were in it for the money. They were running a crooked business and stealing from honest people in town. Anyone who stood in their way got hanged. Sid had been the one to do their dirty work. The problem was, Sid found out what was going on and refused to hang more innocent men. That's why they hired me -- to hang Sid. But Sid was a friend of mine. We'd been trained by the same man. So when the time came to hang Sid, I cut the rope. So Jim -- that was his name -- Jim hanged us both. Well, when it came time for Jim to die, he was an old, sick man. And it would seem that with all the innocent people he'd killed that my services wouldn't have even been needed. The problem was he'd done some good things after he got rich. He helped a lot of poor children -- mostly orphans of his tyranny. So Jim's case wasn't so clear cut and I was called to judge. You should have seen his face when he saw me. There I was, still young and handsome, and he was an old, withered skeleton of a man. To weigh his fate, I asked him a simple question, "Do you regret snapping my neck?"

His eyes opened in fear as he realized he'd hanged his judge. "Yes, I regret snapping your neck. I regret every evil thing I've ever done. Please Lord, take me into heaven."

And in that minute, I knew he lied. His final lie tipped the balance. "Absalom!" I called and my horned friend rose from the bowels of Hell to cart away Jim's soul. I remember smiling as Jim's simple fear transformed to understanding, then to terror.

Clear-cut decisions are the most satisfying. It's the borderline cases that tightened my skin across the bones and blanched it gray. I remember one woman named Rhonda. She sang in the choir of her church, spent her weekends feeding the homeless, and adopted children when she'd find them all alone on the streets. It was one of those homeless kids that caused me to get involved. Trixie was the little girl's name. Trixie had been on the streets since she was five. She was thirteen when Rhonda found her huddled against the wall with a bottle of Jack Daniels pressed against her breasts for warmth. An ice storm was coming and it was cold outside. Rhonda convinced Trixie to go back home with her and sit by the warm fire. She fed her soup, put the bottle of Jack Daniels on the shelf, and wrapped her in a fleece blanket. Trixie fell asleep by the fire and slept for four days. When she woke up, Rhonda brushed out her hair, taught her to read, and treated her like a daughter for two years. Then one day Trixie was walking from the library to the church to meet Rhonda and a man jumped out from behind a building, held her at knifepoint, and raped her. He carved a little gang sign in her thigh and left her bleeding on the street. Trixie was a strong kid. She got herself up and walked to the church, forcing back tears. Well, Rhonda could tell something was wrong and she drew the story out of Trixie. Rhonda held her close and let her cry, silently vowing revenge on the man who raped her.

When the cut on Trixie's thigh healed and left a scar, Rhonda pressed an ink pad against it and stamped it on a piece of paper. She stopped feeding the homeless on the weekends. Instead, she drove around town looking at gang graffiti. After she found the pattern, she kept a vigil on the wall where it was drawn. One by one, the gang members came to draw their mark. One by one, she shot them in cold blood. *For Trixie*, she'd spray on the wall. The police figured a rival gang was responsible and turned their heads. One night, a gang member drove by Rhonda painting on the wall and shot her down.

I came to weigh her evil against her good. Eleven children rescued from the streets. Twelve gang members shot down, but four of those twelve had never killed another. I called a fledgling from the depths of hell. As he approached, Rhonda recognized his tattoo as the mark she'd drawn in her mind hundreds of times -- for Trixie. She gasped as she recognized his soul for what it was. "For Trixie," I whispered in her ear. "This is Nathan Johnson, the man you've hunted all these years. He took his own miserable life shortly after raping Trixie. Ironic, isn't it." I couldn't help but smile at the irony of it. Rhonda didn't smile back. "It's a long walk up the stairs, Rhonda. Tell him about your life and Trixie's. I'm sure he'll want to know. And Nathan, tell Rhonda about the people she killed. The two of you share the blame in their deaths." I followed behind as the two of them ascended the miles of stone stairs. It was the first time I'd ascended the stairs and it would be Nathan Johnson's last. I listened as Rhonda recounted the story of Trixie and told of the gang members she'd shot down. Nathan knew most of her victims and told her about their lives and their families. By the time we reached the top of the stairs, tears were streaming down Rhonda's face. "I'm sorry," she said. "I really thought I was doing good."

"I know." I patted her shoulder and pushed her toward the gate. "That's why you're here and he's there." I pushed Nathan Johnson off the stairs and watched his fledgling wings try to slow his descent. We stood together silently until his scream was silenced by the distance. The gates opened up and Rhonda stepped through them into the waiting arms of her real family and the adopted children who'd come before her.

In the distance, I saw my own twin brother weeping. I saw he was alone and wondered why he was crying if this was heaven. I wondered, not for the first time, if I could have saved him. He was murdered, you see, along with my mother and father. I'd hid under the bed, not making a sound until the thieves took everything we owned and left the house. They never even knew I was there. I crawled out from under the bed and looked briefly at the three corpses I'd called my family. I walked out of the house, alone and young and vengeful. I hadn't learned to be even yet. In the years that followed, I killed to survive. I killed to help others. I killed to get even. It was only after I met Sid that I learned to weigh the good against the bad.

The hardest are the uncompleted souls -- a soul that crosses back and forth between life and death, each time teetering a little closer to one edge or the other. It is my job to watch them balance and to help them decide. In most cases, those who teeter have a wife or husband or child who can't say goodbye. Those are the souls who look at me with fear.

"Souls like mine?" Tony asked.

"You don't look at me with fear, Tony." Bill smiled sardonically. "You look at me and see yourself -- a perfect balance of good and evil."

"I don't want to die," Tony said.

60

"You made that choice hours ago. Too much time has passed to save your life. The problem is, you don't tip the scales in either direction. Save a life, take a life. It's an even balance. I can either flip a coin or..."

"Or?"

"Or you can take my job. I'm tired. It's time for an angel to lift me heavenward. You'd be good at the job. What do you say?"

"Are you sure I can't live? Can't you call for help and let me live?"

"You're dead already, Tony. The only question now is about your soul. What'll it be? Take a chance on fate or live forever as a hangman?" Bill twirled a coin between his fingers.

"You think I'd be good at it?"

"Take my hand, Tony. Press it against your head and let the cold logic seep through you. You'll be great."

Tony felt Bill's coldness enter his head, penetrate his brain, and fill his bloodless hands. Cold, hard logic. He grew confident and strong. This wouldn't be so bad. Tony sat up and opened his eyes. The gray-skinned specter was nowhere to be seen. Maybe it had all been a dream. Tony looked down and saw an icy white line running up his wrist. Blood was still smeared pink around it. He held a black rock in his hand. For some reason, it gave him the willies. He dropped it on the ground.

"It wasn't a dream, Tony." A voice spoke above him. He looked up. Light beams of a hundred colors came together in a point of white light. It reminded him of experiments with prisms in school. A man-like shape descended, becoming more solid as it reached the ground.

"Who are you?" Tony asked.

"My name was Sid," the man said. "I was the other hangman."

"So, hangmen do go to heaven."

Sid reached down and picked up the black rock.

Tony looked skyward and then back to the angel. "What about Bill? Is Bill in heaven?"

"From dust he rose and to dust he doth return." Sid crumbled the black rock in his hands, watching the pieces fall onto the white linoleum floor. "Dust," he said. "Just dust."

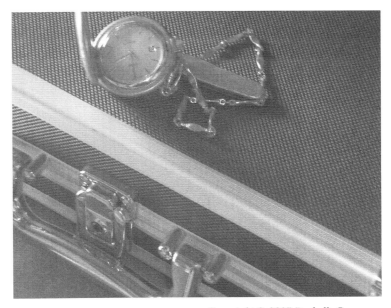

His Last Shot

By John E. Miller

In the early summer morning hours, Lance drove down the empty highway, the heater of his car turned down to low, in hopes that it would dry off his clothes. He didn't need the warmth. It was one of those warm summer rains and as he drove, the windshield wipers kept time to the music on the radio. Every so often Lance caught himself watching the wipers swing back and forth across his windshield. Pay attention, he reprimanded himself. "Always keep your eyes on the road," his grandfather had told him a long time ago when he'd taught him how to drive. Lance glanced over to the passenger's seat briefly, not wanting to see the two by two foot red strongbox and the gold watch resting on top of it.

Lance thought back on what had happened at his job earlier that evening. It had started out routine. Disabling the alarm system and phone line was a breeze. He had a Master's degree in electronics and he had written his thesis on security systems. The home was a nice suburban home, widely spaced from the neighbors by a large yard. As Lance had entered the home, he had noted that it was well kept. It was Lance's habit to notice how the home was kept. Mr. Arthur Downs either had a wife who was a clean freak or they had a maid. Either way, someone was bound to be upset about the white carpet if things got messy. But then things rarely got messy. As he moved towards the steps leading upstairs to the bedrooms, Lance noticed a picture on the wall out of the corner of his eye. He recognized the man in the photo. It was a picture of Mr. Downs and a young boy who must have been his grandson holding up the catch of the day. Of course Mr. Downs was holding the smaller fish. Lance heard the chamber of a shotgun loading.

"Who the hell are you and how did you get in my house?" a loud, but frightened voice asked.

Lance looked up the stairs and saw Mr. Downs holding a shotgun in his hand. He had not put it up to his shoulder yet, but Lance knew he had only one chance to make his shot. He pulled his pistol from the shoulder holster inside his suit jacket and fired. The shot was silent, but hit its mark. Mr. Downs' shotgun broke apart, as its firing pin fell to the ground.

Mr. Downs looked down at his gun. Lance still smiled, remembering the surprise on the old man's face.

"I did not come to rob you, Mr. Downs," Lance spoke calmly. "I came here to kill you."

Now

Lance saw a sign flicker alive up ahead. He could barely make it out between the raindrops, but he was pretty sure it read "Lady Queen." It looked like some kind of diner. He pulled into the parking lot just as he saw the orange and white blinds rolled up. It had been years since he'd been in a small hometown café, but he could still remember the smell of fried food, toast, bacon, syrup, and coffee mingled with stale cigarette smoke and freshly pressed newsprint. He remembered many Sunday mornings sitting at a diner, watching his grandfather read the paper. First the local news, then the obituaries, and then the front page news. "What's going on in the world doesn't matter much," he'd say. "But it doesn't hurt to be educated about it." He'd always saved the funnies for last.

Lance got out of his car and walk up to the diner's door. The door was unlocked. Good, it was open. He stepped into a narrow entryway and wiped off his feet. Then he opened the second door and walked in.

"We've got coffee, but the iron isn't hot yet," a deep friendly voice called out from the kitchen.

"That's fine, I'll have some coffee," Lance replied. "Coffee?" he thought to himself. He hadn't had coffee in years. He'd always worried that it would make him jumpy. He walked to a window booth and looked out the window at the rain. He put the box and the pocket watch on the table and sat down.

A young waitress brought out a cup and a pot of coffee. She poured Lance a cup and walked away with a smile, leaving behind some sugar packets and a creamer of half and half. As she walked away Lance thought how pretty her long brown hair was and how nicely she moved in her faded blue jeans. He wondered if the jeans were faded with age or if she'd bought them that way. He sipped his coffee and remembered a night in the early eighties.

1982 (or thereabouts)

A freshman at college, Lance didn't know too many people. Well, really he just knew one, his friend Paul. Paul had invited him to a party at a friend's house. Lance had said no at first because he didn't drink, but Paul had convinced him to go, if only to make sure he'd make it home alive.

Once at the party Lance got himself a large glass of tea and sat at one end of the couch. He watched in silence as the people at the party drank and started acting silly. Suddenly his view was blocked by two pair of faded jeans.

"Which are real and which were bought faded?" a light voice asked.

"What?" asked Lance.

"The jeans! Which pair is faded by time and which was faded by the manufacturer?" the pretty girl with long flowing dark hair leaned toward him. Lance realized she was flirting with him.

"If I guess right what do I win?" he asked.

"Maybe a chance to get into one of the pair of jeans?" the young lady with the long hair giggled.

Lance looked at the girls. Both of them were very attractive to Lance; one had long flowing dark hair and the other had short red hair. Both were dressed nice, but Lance could tell that the long haired girl's shirt was slightly out of date. The redhead wore a shirt that still smelled new. Factory-washed, not home laundered. Lance looked into the eyes of the long-haired girl and said softly, "I would say that yours are the true faded jeans."

"You're good," she said and sat down beside Lance.

Lance smiled and put his arm around her. They hardly noticed the redhead move off to the dance floor.

Now

"My name is Alice. Are you ready to order?"

Lance looked up from his coffee at the pair of faded jeans, down at the white Formica table, then up again, remembering where he was. The young waitress stood next to him with a pencil and pad of paper.

"I'm sorry. I didn't know that you were lost in thought." Alice said. "I didn't mean to interrupt."

"Interrupt? No, that's okay. I need to quit doing that. Now what did you say?"

"What would you like to order?"

Lance looked down at the menu and saw the Trucker Special in big bold letters. Only $5.95. "I'll have the Trucker Special."

Alice looked at him quizzically. "Okay, but if you don't mind me saying, you don't look like a man who would eat that type of meal."

"You're right," he smiled. "I'm doing a lot of things today I don't usually do."

Alice wrote down the order and started walking off. "And a large glass of orange juice, please." Lance called after her.

Alice nodded her head.

Lance took a sip of his coffee. For a small town restaurant, the coffee was quite good. Too strong for him, since this was the first cup he'd had in over twenty years, but good. He added a bit of cream. Evaporated milk was what his grandfather had put in his coffee. Not when they were out, but when he was at home. Lance remembered the white and red can covered with aluminum foil always in the corner of the refrigerator.

Two old men walked in from a different set of doors and set opposite of each other without saying a word. Alice walked over to them, poured them each a cup of coffee, and wrote on her order pad. Not a word was exchanged.

"Regulars, I guess." Lance thought to himself.

One of the old men noticed Lance looking their way. Lance smiled and gave a nod. The old man said something and his friend turned to look at Lance. Again, Lance smiled and nodded his head. The old men lost interest and turned back to face each other silently.

"Sorry to surprise you men," Lance thought.

Lance remembered his grandfather telling him that he still went to the old diner with his friends. Every Sunday morning, just like he used to do with Lance before he'd gone away to college. So long ago.

Lance looked around the café and noticed little knick-knacks on the wall like you would see in an old 1950's movie. Lance could not remember the last time that he had seen a movie. His eyes traveled past the knick-knacks to a picture of a man sitting by a black bear. He held the bear's head up with one hand and cradled a bow in the other. Lance grinned. Somebody must be a hunter. In a different life he and that man might have hunted together.

1982 (or thereabouts)

"Okay son," the coach looked over the certificates and smiled up at him. "You say you want to join the archery club. I see you have won quite a few competitions."

Lance smiled, "My grandfather loves to shoot a bow. One day, when he can spare the time off work, we plan to go bear hunting."

"Hmmmm…" the coach shook his head. "Look, I'm sorry son, but you're a freshman and you haven't taken my class yet… I wish I could do something for you, but rules are rules."

Lance looked sadly at the bows hung neatly on the wall, "I was afraid you would say that. Next year maybe?"

"Maybe," the coach patted him on the shoulder. "Sign up for my course."

Lance started to walk away. He felt hurt, but knew there was no reason for it. He was just feeling lost. He didn't know anyone yet. That's all. He'd meet people in his classes. Still, archery was one thing he knew he was good at. This other stuff, he wasn't so sure.

A kid about his age with black hair ran up to the coach. "Coach… Coach… I've got an idea. Why don't we take him out to the range and if he is as good as us or better, you let him on the team? You can get his P.E. class changed to yours."

Lance stopped walking. His ears perked up hopefully, like a fox listening to the call of a guinea hen separated from her pack.

"Housener, you know I can't do that. Class schedules are already set. Besides, he's a freshman."

"Coach. We lost Dead Shot when he graduated and Long Bow started his residency this year. So he will be at the hospital all the time."

The coach thought for a moment. "Alright, we'll try him. But if he does well and I let him join, he's your responsibility. Got me?"

"Alright," Housener hooted and walked over to Lance. "You heard the man! You've got one shot. I'm Paul Housener, by the way."

"Lance Corporal," Lance smiled. "Good to meet you."

Paul Housener leaned over and whispered, "You fuck this up and you're a dead man, Lance."

Lance nodded and thought, "Great. First day here and I have either made a friend for life or a mortal enemy."

The coach grabbed one of the new composite bows with pulls and weights.

"No.... Coach if he wants to be on the team he must do it the hard way, give him one of the old style composite bows."

The coach shrugged and handed Lance one of the old style bows and some graphite arrows.

"You don't have any with a wood shaft?" Lance asked.

Housener looked at Lance questioningly, "It's your funeral."

The three of them walked out to the range. They stepped up to the pad twenty-five feet from the target. Lance aimed and shot, hitting in the red zone.

"That was only twenty-five feet," said the coach. "Let's see what you can do at 50."

Lance stepped out to fifty feet and shot again. Once again it landed in the red zone. Then 75 and 100. His final shot was at 300 feet.

The coach shook his head. "I don't think that bow can reach a target that far out."

"Let him try, Coach," Housener was clearly excited and impressed.

Lance pulled the arrow back, angled it high in the air, and shot. The arrow seemed to hang in the air a long time, but when it hit, it was in the red zone.

The coach's mouth dropped wide open. Lance smiled.

"How did you do that?" Housener asked.

"I'm used to the old bows and the wood shaft arrows. They're all my grandfather would let me use. I started shooting when I was six."

"Well?" Housener asked, nudging the coach.

The coach laughed, "Alright he's on the team."

The coach walked off shaking his head. The boys could tell he was smiling.

"Friend or foe?" Lance asked, holding his right hand out to Paul.

"Friend that's for sure... But how did you do that?"

Lance felt his smile slouch off his face, "I think of that rich bastard who killed my grandmother and got off Scott free because he had money." He walked over to the hanger for the bows and put it up.

He never noticed Housener smiling, but now looking back, Lance was pretty sure he was.

Now

"More coffee, Sir?" Alice asked.

Lance snapped out of his thought, "Sorry?!"

"Would you like more coffee?"

Lance nodded and she filled his cup.

"Do you hunt?" she asked. "I couldn't help noticing that you were looking at my boss' bear hunting picture."

"I used to. I was pretty good with a bow," Lance smiled. "But I've have given it up."

She smiled and walked off.

December 4th, 1982

It had been raining and cold for a week. Target practice had already been called off twice that week and it was likely it would be called off tomorrow from the looks of things. The rain had started turning icy when they left the cafeteria after dinner.

Now Housener was in Lance's room and they were working on homework. It was nearly finals time and Lance was feeling the stress. They were both deep in concentration when the phone rang. Lance jumped a little and picked it up. "Hello? Uncle Tim? Why are you calling?"

Lance listened, feeling his fingers clench the phone. He saw Housener glance up from his book and lift an eyebrow.

"Is he okay? Not worry? Shit, a stroke can be a dangerous thing."

Housener mouthed, 'Grandfather?' and Lance nodded.

"Tell him not to worry about me. I have a job and I can get more student loans. How is Granddad going to pay for this…? No… No… I'll find another job and help him. I know if you could you would. Alright, Uncle Tim. Tell him I love him."

Lance hung up the phone with a long face..

Housener reached across the table and put his hand on Lance's arm, "Sorry, dude. I didn't mean to eavesdrop. Is your grandfather okay?"

Lance sat in silence for a moment, staring at his open book. Then he looked up at Housener, "Yeah, he's a real trooper."

Housener nodded. "And I couldn't help overhearing you're hurting for cash."

"I'll make it," Lance lifted Housener's hand off his arm. "I can always get another job."

"I think I know of a job right up your alley," Housener smiled and grasped Lance's hand in a firm handshake. "Welcome to the new world."

Lance shook his friend's hand and noticed for the first time that Housener's eyes were almost grey. Like steel.

Now

Lance noticed Alice looking his way as she poured the two old men some more coffee. He thought he even saw her blush a little as she walked over toward him.

"Coffee?"

"No, but I would like some grapefruit juice if you don't mind."

She raised an eyebrow.

"Some wrong Alice?"

"You don't look like a grapefruit man"

73

"My grandfather and I drank it all the time," Lance smiled and nodded toward the two old men. "And by the way, I'll pay for their ticket."

"Are you sure?"

"Sure as rain, as my grandfather would say." Lance winked.

She smiled and walks off. The older gentlemen got up and walked up to the cash register to pay their bill. Alice whispered something to them and they looked over at Lance. Lance smiled and nodded.

The two older gentlemen walked toward the set of doors near Lance. Before leaving, one stopped to shake Lance's hand. "Thank you. You're a good man."

The man's hand was spotted with age as his grandfather's had been the last time he'd been to visit. Lance returned the handshake and smiled.

Last winter

It was a cold winter morning with a fair chance of snow in Manhattan. Lance hated to fly, but when it came to work, he would do what was needed. He just hoped he would not get snowed in. He had all the information he needed in his briefcase – a full dossier on the client and the job. He always insisted on as much detail as possible. He also carried an umbrella.

Lance had called his grandfather the night before to tell him he had some work to do in New York and he would not be able to call him for a few days. He had heard a rumbling in his grandfather's voice that bothered him. He offered to postpone going to New York, but his grandfather told him it was just a cold. Lance should have known better.

Lance took a cab to Washington Square Park. The job was in one of those villages that you heard about on television. Lance could never understand how there could be a village in New York City.

He looked around and compared his surroundings with what the client had described. He knew he was in the right neighborhood because the description matched down to cracks in the sidewalk. He found the deli and noted its name in big bold Hebrew letters, with a smaller translation in English. Lance checked his watch -- 3:15 New York time and, like clockwork, two elderly men walked into the deli, sat opposite of each other in the front window and started to play chess. He loved when his information was so accurate.

Lance walked into the deli and passed the table where the old men sat. He can't remember what he said he tripped over when he hit Mr. Sheldon Goldstein in the arm with his umbrella. Lance kept moving up to the counter and ordered a bagel. Mr. Goldstein was still cussing at him when he left. Lance walked three blocks before catching a cab and had it take him to the train station. From there, he'd catch another cab to the airport. He looked at his watch -- 3:45, by this time Mr. Goldstein would be having a heart attack.

Crash!

Now

Lance jumped a bit as Alice lay his large breakfast in front of him. He looked down at all the food: four eggs, four patties of sausages, six linked sausages, two slices of ham, a dinner bowl of biscuits and gravy, a bowl of grits, six pancakes, four pieces of toast and a large glass of orange juice. Lance looked up at Alice, pleadingly, "You're not hungry by any chance?"

Alice laughed, "I told you it might be too much."

"Oh I could eat that and more," a small voice spoke from behind Alice.

"Jimmy, don't bother the man."

"It's okay, really," Lance looked behind Alice and saw a young boy. His build was slight -- even a light wind would blow him over. He had dark hair like his mother and a wide buck-toothed grin. "So sport, you think you can eat this much and more?"

"Yep."

"I'm sorry. My son gets carried away some times," Alice apologized again.

Lance looked at Alice and then back at her son. It looked like they had both missed a few meals. "I'll tell you what. If your mother doesn't mind and will bring an extra plate over, I'll share with you. And if you are still hungry when we're finished, I'll buy whatever you want."

"Mister you don't have…"

"Look, Alice, you and I both know I'll never be able to eat all of this. I would hate for it to go to waste. I won't hurt your son. He will be right here where you can see him. Really, it's more of a favor for me than him or you. It'll give me someone to talk to."

Alice looked from Lance to her son's 'please mom' smile on his face. "Alright, but if he becomes a bother chase him back to me."

Alice walked to her son and leaned over and whispered something to him. Then she picked up a clean a plate and escorted Jimmy to Lance's table. "Jimmy I would like you to meet…."

"Lance. Lance Corporal," Lance smiled and held out his hand. "I'm down here for the telephone company looking for places to put in wireless towers."

Jimmy shook his hand and sat down. Without saying a word, he started to load his plate.

"Jimmy you should ask Mr. Corporal first."

"But he already invited me to eat."

"Still…"

"It's okay, Alice. We'll be fine."

"I'll pay half," Alice said, quiet but firm.

"Why!? My company pays for it."

Alice stood up and smiled.

"So Jimmy, why are you dressed up for school? Too many snow days?" Lance put another piece of bacon and some sausage onto Jimmy's plate.

"No. I go to summer school."

"You look like a bright young man to need summer school."

Jimmy laughed. "Summer school isn't only for the kids who have problems in school. It's for everyone who wants to take it. I wanted to take it this summer for the science fair."

"Oh, I see," Lance dipped his toast in the yellow of his egg and put it to his mouth.

April 19th, 1972

"Nan Nu, are you going to come and see my science fair project today?"

"I wouldn't miss it for the world, Sport," his grandmother tousled his hair.

Lance grinned. He could not finished his breakfast fast enough. He wanted to get to school and show off his science project. *Computers and how they will change our world.* Lance was proud of himself. He did all the work himself. He drew all of the pictures, and even learned some BASIC programming on his own.

"I'll show them. Show them all that I'm not a loser," Lance thought to himself.

"Okay, Sport. Let's go," his grandmother put his Lunar Landing lunchbox on the table.

Lance finished eating, then picked up his plate, took it to the sink, and rinsed it off.

Lance's grandmother stood at the back door, holding the screen door open. She smiled proudly at her grandson. Lance took his grandmother's hand and they walked out the door.

Lance's grandmother walked him to school every day. The other kids teased him about it, but he didn't mind. He got to spend some special time with his grandmother. Just him and her. It wasn't at all like the time he had to do with his mother. And who the hell knew about his father. "And who really gave a shit?" Lance would often think. But he wasn't thinking about that today. He knew he had the science fair in the bag.

"Nan Nu do you think Granddad will make it?" Lance knew the answer before his grandmother told him.

"I'm sorry, Sport. Your Granddad is much too busy to come, but he did say he would be home early."

"I know. I just kind of hoped he would." It was too bad that his grandfather had to work; it always seemed like his grandfather had to work. He would get up before dawn and would not be home until after dark. He made explosives and by-products.

"You know if he could make it, he would. But I can tell you this, when you bring home that blue ribbon, he will have three or four buttons broken off of his work shirt for weeks."

Lance smiled a wide grin and swung his grandmother's hand happily as they walked. The walk was a short one. The school was only two blocks from the house. It was springtime. The road was lined with mulberry trees just starting to bud. Lance and his grandmother talked about the trees coming to life and the way spring smelled – new and sweet like fresh strawberries covered in cream. Lance and his grandmother loved spring and fall, but this spring was the best. Granddad didn't have to work late and Lance was a shoe-in for the science fair. Besides, he was sure he had smelled a grapefruit pie in the oven when he woke up.

They crossed the last street and Lance saw Greg waiting for him. They were an odd pairing for the science fair. Lance hadn't been chosen by his own classmates, so he'd asked if Greg, a student a year below him could help him with his project. The teacher had no problem with this. It was a small town and everyone knew that Lance and Greg were the best of friends.

Lance raced over to Greg so they could go over the final notes of their science project. Lance's grandmother crossed, not running but not walking because she worried about her grandson's safety. A car came out of nowhere. Lance looked back when he heard the brakes squeal, just in time to see his grandmother's body slam against a mulberry tree and land motionless in a bed of bright red tulips. Lance's world went into slow motion as he watched the driver, eyes burning red and drunken, lips moving silently. Lance ran toward his grandmother's broken body and the driver revved his engine and drove away.

December 10th, 1982

"You want to talk about a bastard, this guy has hit more than twenty people," Housener told Lance.

Lance sat next to Housener in the limo, quietly eyeing the guy who Housener called Ace.

"Can he do it?" asked Ace.

"He's your best shot," said Housener. "For this guy, he's your only shot."

"You'd best be right or you're both dead," Ace held his hand in the shape of a pistol and raised it to Housener's head.

Housener didn't even blink. "Don't worry. Coldsnap has it covered."

"He'd better." Ace laid down 50,000 dollars, fanned out like a hand of cards.

Lance stomach turned as he looked at the money, "I thought the gig was for 150,000."

Housener whispered "Dude, take the money"

Ace looked down at the money, "Problem?"

Lance smiled, "The gig was for a 150,000."

Ace spoke slowly, as if to a foreigner, "Do you have a problem?"

Lance heard his own voice, cold and steady, "Yes, I do."

Housener whispered "Take the money."

"No," Lance whispered, "Welcome to the new world."

Ace sat back in the seat, "And what is this?"

Lance smiled, knowing he had won his hand, "I'm doing the hunting, so I should get the better half."

Ace shrugs, "What's your price?"

Lance looked Ace in the eye, "60/40 works for me, I get the 60."

Ace looked at Housener, who bowed away, "You do the job and you have your price."

Lance sat quietly for a few moments, staring at the cash on the seat of the limo. Finally, he spoke, "Money first and then the job."

Housener's mouth dropped wide open.

"I'll give you this, kid...You were raised with some balls... Alright you've got a deal."

Housener just shook his head. Ace pulled out some more money, and then looked at Housener. "Well, show him the doc on the guy, Housener."

Housener pulled out a folder. Printed on it was one word, 'BEAR'.

"You're going to like this one, Lance."

Lance looked over the documents for a few minutes, wondering why he needed to know so much about a man whose life was about to end. Then one fact caught his eye. Bear had been arrested for drunk driving and manslaughter, but all charges were dropped. Lance took his time going over the paperwork.

"How do you want me to go about this?"

"Well the Bear like to have a smoke and some coffee around six a.m., and then he will do some stretches by the golf course."

Lance looked at his watch and thought, "5:30, not giving me much time." But he nodded and got out of the limo. Lance walked across the golf course and noticed how well-kept the grass was. Finally, he reached an old oak tree. There was the Bear about 200 feet away, doing his stretches just like they said he would be.

"This one is for my grandmother and any other grandmother you may have killed... Murderer." Lance raised his bow and let the arrow fly. He didn't have to look, for he knew he would hit his mark, but he watched just the same to make sure the Bear dropped. Quietly, like the arrow that downed him. Lance walked calmly back to the limo.

Now

"I guess you're right. My eyes were bigger than my stomach."

Lance looked across the table at Jimmy and smiled, "I guess my eyes were too big also."

Jimmy laughed and got up from the table. He started heading over to his mother, then stopped and turned to Lance, "Thanks mister. Oh, by the way, my mom's not married."

"Jimmy!" Alice yelled.

Lance laughed despite himself.

"It's true, Mom. You're not married."

"Still, you don't need to tell everyone."

"But he's not married. I know because I looked at his hand and he has no ring on it."

"Jimmy please, I think you should run along and get to school."

"Will you be here when I get out of school?"

"I don't know. I have to see what the day brings. Stop by here first."

Jimmy grabbed his school items and ran out the door.

Alice walked toward Lance and started to pick up the plates, "I'm sorry about that, sir. Do you need a carryout box?"

"Lance," Lance looked at Alice's slender fingers. "Please, call me Lance. And no."

She smiled, "Lance." Then she turned and walked away, balancing the plates on one arm.

Lance couldn't help looking at her ass in those faded blue jeans. Alice happened to glance back, and when she saw Lance looking at her, she blushed.

Lance smiled at her and winked.

1983 (or thereabouts)

Lance watched Linda slowly walking away. He still could feel the tears on his shoulder. "Her ass always looked good in those jeans, but it was the right thing to do," Lance reassured himself. She was getting too close, asking too many questions. He had to let her go. It was for her own good. The jobs Lance had been taking lately had become much more dangerous. If anyone found out they were dating, they might put a hit on her.

Lance watched her merge into the mass of students going to and from class. Then he walked over to his car.

There was really no choice in the matter. He had to take these new jobs, with his grandfather being as sick as he had been. "Yes, this was for the best."

He opened the car door, climbed inside, and drove away.

Now

A bright reflection caught Lance's eye as he watched a police officer walk into the restaurant. Lance took a sip of his coffee. The officer nodded in his general direction, then took a seat nearby. Lance wondered if Mr. Downs had changed his mind.

"It doesn't really matter at this point" Lance told himself.

Lance watched the officer out of the corner of his eye. Alice took the officer's order and walked off. After she turned the order in, she walked toward Lance, "Would you like anything else?"

"Not right now. Is it alright if I just sit here for a bit?"

"Sure. It's a slow day. Take all the time you need. Would you like some water?"

"Water would be good. Thanks."

Alice brought him his water, then turned to leave. He put his hand on her elbow.

"Yes. Mr…. Lance?"

"The officer over there -- has he paid his bill yet?"

"No. Why?"

"I would like to take care of it for him."

"You're a very giving person."

"No, not really. My grandfather was. He and my grandmother raised me."

Alice smiled, "Be right back."

In a few moments Alice walked back with a plate, "Mind if I join you?"

"Not at all...Please have a seat."

Alice sat down with some tea and a sandwich. "How long are you going to be in town?"

"Just the day." Lance gave her a small half grin, "Why?"

"Well, I was going to say that you could come over and have a home cooked meal and maybe watch a DVD."

He smiles, "That is awful tempting... I'll tell you what... If for some reason I'm in town overnight, then I would love to come over."

Alice blushed a bit and said softly, "That would be nice."

As Lance watched her eat, he noticed how small and delicate her hands were.

"You have lovely hands."

"Thank you... Did you know I could read palms?"

"No I didn't."

"Would you like me to read yours?"

"Sure."

She took Lance's hand into hers. He had forgotten how soft a woman's hand could be.

Kindergarten

"Students, I'd like you to meet Officer MacAfee. Officer MacAfee will be taking our fingerprints for the school records."

"Thank you Miss Thomas. Now children, you will see today how each of us has a very different fingerprint. I will be rolling your index finger tip in a special ink and then rolling it on the card. After I'm done, you will compare your fingerprint to someone else's print and we will see how different they really are. Okay, now who is first on my list? Sandy Baker would you come up please?"

A girl with curly red hair stepped up and the officer fingerprinted her.

"Okay, Robert Blossom, you're next." He pressed the child's finger in the ink and then on the card.

"Lance Corporal. Come up please." Lance hesitated before walking to the front. The officer rolled his finger in the ink and then on the card. As Lance started to go, the officer looked at the sheet. He pulled Lance back and examined his fingertips, then looked at the card again. He wiped the ink from Lance's fingertip, "Well I'll be damn!" He whispered to Lance, "It's alright son, go sit down."

The Officer turned to everyone. "Let's see what we have. Here is Sally's fingerprint." He put her card under an overhead projector, and then he set Robert's card by hers. "See, children, how the prints are different. We call the lines 'road maps' and the blanks 'ditches'. Now here is a special treat for you. Something I've never seen in all my years on the force." The officer put Lance's fingerprints under the other two.

"Now, can anyone tell me what is different about Lance's fingerprint?"

The officer nodded at one of the children with a raised hand. "It's all black," the child said.

"Right, so this means that either Lance is a robot or an alien or he is one of very few people who doesn't have fingerprints." All of the kids in the class started to laugh. Except Lance. It took Lance three years and several fights before the other kids quit calling him 'Mr. Robot Head' or "My Stupid Martian."

"Now really kids, the downside of this is that he can't hold things as easily as us, but on the other hand he could..."

Now

"Murder!"

Lance snaps out of his haze "What?"

"You could either rob a bank or commit murder because you don't have fingerprints," Alice marveled over his smooth fingertips. "Sorry, I just noticed."

"Yes, I guess I could," Lance felt a shiver run up his spine. "So, what did you say about my palm?"

"Oh, you have a long sex drive," Alice blushed. "But it shows a short life." She dropped his hand down suddenly, "You shouldn't worry about these things. It's not real after all."

Lance looked at his hand and thought, "More real than you know."

"Well my break's over," Alice stood up from the table. "Back to work"

Lance nodded his head and watched her walk away.

Earlier

"Who wants me dead?" Mr. Downs asked, pouring himself a drink. He took a large swallow and shook his glass. "Want one?"

"Please. Something light. I have never had a drink before."

"In your line of work, I would have thought it a necessary part of the job."

"For some…..Yes….. I always like to keep my head clear."

Mr. Downs handed Lance a drink and sat in a big chair. Lance pulled out a folder and handed it to Mr. Downs.

"What's this?"

"It's your folder. Everything about you, your wife, your family and your business. The contract lays out the whole thing. They wanted you and your wife out of the picture so they could put your son-in-law in your place."

"Do you know if he's behind any of this?"

"If he is, he's just a yes man"

Mr. Down looked over the paper and nodded, "You're very thorough."

"It's my job."

"Why are you giving me this?"

"You're free."

"Free?"

"Yes. Yours is only contract I will not finish."

"Why?"

"I quit….. Do what you will with the information."

"I haven't been in big business this long to know that a person never just quits. I'm curious. What's your reason?"

"Alright, I'll tell you. I saw the picture of you and your grandson. It reminded me of my grandfather and I…. He died yesterday."

"I'm sorry to hear that."

Lance looked at him coldly and shrugged his shoulders, "People die."

Mr. Down nodded, "I guess in your line of work, you become callous about death. You'd have to if you wanted to keep on doing it."

"Yes, I guess you're right… I'll deactivate my jam if you'd like to call the police."

"After you leave."

Lance finished his drink and set the glass down, "Thank you, Mr. Downs."

"I will be calling the police, but not for you." He held up the paperwork.

Lance nodded, walked out to his car, and drove away.

Now

A young woman who Lance thought looked like she should still be in school walked in with a little girl and took the booth by the door. The little girl scooted over to the large window, knelt on the bench and stared out of it.

"Jenny, please sit down."

"Okay, Mommy."

Lance looked at the young woman again. She certainly didn't look old enough to be Jenny's mother.

"Now remember, Jenny. We can't get a whole lot."

"I know."

Alice started to walk over to them, but Lance caught her eye, and she walked to his table first. "Let me guess. It's on you."

Lance just smiled.

Alice smiled back, shaking her head. She walked over to the young mother's table and leaned over to whisper to the mother.

Lance played with his gold watch and pretended not to notice the young lady look over his way.

He glanced down at the watch and thought, "2:15. I didn't realize it had gotten that late."

Yesterday

"Mr. Corporal, glad you could make it," the older man shook his hand.

"Call me Lance. Please."

"Ok, Lance. Of course you know why you are here. I wish it were under better circumstances."

"I understand. It's alright. He lived a full life. They did all they could do to stop the cancer."

The older man shook his head, "Cancer is a terrible thing." He put a red box and a watch on the counter.

"What's this?"

"This is what he left you. Everything else went to your uncle Tim or to the church. If you want to contest it, I can give you the necessary paperwork."

"No, that's alright. That's how he wanted things. Thank you anyway. May I have a look?"

"By all means, here is the key."

Lance opened the box and looked down on stacks of hundred dollar bills and neatly folded news clippings.

"Is there something wrong, Lance?" The attorney looked concerned. "It's all there, $1.25 million. It's what he said was yours."

"No, everything's fine."

"I hate to bring it up, but he didn't leave anything for my fees."

Lance took his checkbook out of his inner jacket pocket, wrote a check, and handed it to the attorney. "Of course. He would have wanted you to have something for your effort."

Lance closed the box, picked it up along with the pocket watch and left the attorney's office.

In the back of the cab, Lance looked at the news clippings from papers around the world. He quickly calculated what he'd earned over the years and what he'd sent. He felt sick to his stomach. The old man hadn't spent a penny of it.

Now

"Lance, do you want anymore coffee?"

"What? Sorry, I was daydreaming again."

"More coffee?"

"Sure."

91

Alice poured the coffee and walked away.

Lance looked at his reflection in the watch. He could swear the man who looked back was an old man, his grandfather. He studied the reflection. "I wondered why you called me less and less. I thought it was because you were sick... You were sick. Sick at who I was." Lance turned the watch over and read the inscription as he'd done repeatedly in the cab, at the airport, and on the flight home. 'A man's greatest wealth is pride in his life's work.'

He saw a tear pool on the watch, distorting the reflection so that it no longer resembled the only man Lance had loved. What looked back at him now was a monstrous man. "He was right... He was always right. I am a monster, a robot, an alien. I took pride in my work. The work of murder. I am no better than that murderer who killed my Nan-nu. He was always right and I miss him."

Lance heard two cars screech outside the window. He looked out and four men in suits stepped out of each car. Housener was the last to step out. He wiped his eye. No time for tears now. "That's right. Bring all of them, Housener. You said I was the best they had and now I know you were right. You know singly I can kill each of you, but as a group you might just have a chance."

Lance picked up the red box and walked over to the counter. "Here's your tip, Alice. And I'll give you one more. Get down NOW! Hell has just reached your town."

Alice looked at him, shocked. Then she saw the men outside. She whispered, "You did murder."

Tears welled up in Lance eyes and he whispered, "Sorry about tonight. I can't make it. I would have loved too, though."

92

"Cookie get down now," screamed Alice. Lance heard the cook drop to the floor. Alice dropped too.

Lance turned calmly and started walking to the door. He stopped by the young woman and child. The young woman looked very frightened. He slowly handed the watch to the child. "Believe in what the watch says Jenny… I didn't… Now both of you get down behind the stone wall and don't get up."

The young woman grabbed Jenny and the both crouched down behind the wall and under the table. Lance pulled out two 9mm guns and walked out the first door; he stood in the little entryway for a moment, took a deep breath, and stepped out the next door.

Alice could not hear her own scream as the shots rang out and broken glass crashed down on the white Formica tables.

Immortal

by John E. Miller

Doctor Feldman walks out of the rain into the foyer. He looks backs at the grey pavement before being buzzed through the final door. He remembers other mornings when the sidewalks were slate white. He thinks about the one day a young man had drawn on them with chalk and out of respect for the young artist, he had walked around the drawings, unlike some of the people in the city who had simply walked over them.

"Ha ha! Good morning, Doc," a familiar voice boomed out from behind the lobby desk.

Feldman winces, but tries not to let it show. He hates the fact that being called "Doc" still sends an icy tremor down his spine. As a doctor, he despises irrationality, especially his own.

"Good morning, Max… New joke?

"No sir, I met your first patient. I'm sorry, but you have a winner on your hands today."

"Now Max, I'm here to help these people. Their sickness is nothing to laugh at."

"I know sir, but he says the funniest things. And he even laughs at himself."

Feldman smiles. "I guess that's good. Is his paperwork here or with Lisa?"

"With Lisa."

"Very good and the patient is in the ready room?"

"Yes. Phil's with him right now and he's been no trouble."

"Good. I'll have Lisa call when I'm ready for him." Feldman turns toward the elevator.

"Yes, Doctor Feldman. Oh by the way, your wife called and said that Billy can get the cast removed today."

Feldman nods.

"So what is that, the third break this year?" Max asks genially.

"Yes. I wish he would take up a safer sport than motor cross racing."

"It could be worse."

"How's that?"

"Oh I don't know, cave diving?"

Feldman chuckles. "Please don't bring that up to him."

"Don't worry, Doc. I won't."

Feldman walks to the elevator and presses Up. When the elevator opens, he steps inside and glances at the buttons. Funny, he'd never noticed before that the contractor was superstitious; he had skipped the 13th floor and made it the 14th. Lucky for Feldman, his office is on the 7th floor.

As he steps out of the elevator, he sees Lisa through the glass walls. He can't figure out know how he let his wife talk him in to having full glass walls in his waiting room. It was only that one time, Feldman reminds himself. Who would have thought a man would freak out about glass walls?

Feldman steps into his empty waiting room.

"Good morning, Lisa. Any calls?"

"Good morning, Dr. Feldman," Lisa looks up from her typing and smiles at him. Just your wife about your son's arm, but I would guess Max already let you know about that."

"Yes he did."

"I put the new patient's paperwork on your desk." She leans toward him slightly and mouths, "Good luck."

Feldman raises an eyebrow, "Is he dangerous?"

"No… but he is out there and it seems that weird things happen around him"

Feldman gives a short snort, "*Weird* things?"

"Yes," she turns back to her typing. "It's all in the report."

"Alright. Could you start some coffee?"

A laugh lit up his receptionist's face. "Oh please Doctor! I already have your coffee made for you. Just like I always do."

Feldman could swear that for the last ten years he had usually made his own coffee, but he smiles. "Why thank you Lisa."

She laughs again, but this time a bit nervous. "You're welcome. Are you okay, Dr. Feldman?"

"Yes," he gives her a puzzled look. "Why would you ask?"

"I don't know. It has been a long time since you thanked me for making coffee. It's always been part of my daily tasks."

"Well I should be more appreciative of the hard work you do."

Lisa glances at her desk calendar to make sure it's not Secretary's Day, then looks her boss over curiously. "Are you sure you're okay?"

Feldman laughs, "Yes, quite." He walks into his office and shuts the door behind him.

Feldman pours himself some coffee from the freshly made pot and sits at his desk. He looks at the picture of his son and wife sitting on the edge of his desk and wonders, not for the first time, how many times the boy will have to break a bone before he learns to be more cautious. Then he takes a sip of coffee, strong and black the way he likes it, and opens the new patient's file.

As he reads the file, Feldman makes mental notes about the case, 'Hears voices, see things, self destructive...Not a difficult diagnosis....classic schizophrenic. Wonder why the state would send the patient his way." He reads on.

"Doctor, are you ready to see your new patient?" Lisa's voice echoes through the speakers on his phone.

Feldman picks up the phone, "Not quite yet, Lisa. Would you come in for moment?"

A few moments later, Lisa opens the door and steps into his office, filling the air of his office with a heavy floral scent. Funny, he didn't remember smelling perfume in the waiting room. She must have put it on after he left.

"Yes Doctor, what is it?" She moved toward his desk.

He turns the file toward her and points to the page. "It says here that he had two other doctors. One committed suicide and the other went on a killing rampage?"

"Yes Doctor. I called and checked on that and it is all true."

"It says both incidents happened during a therapy session."

"Yes Doctor, all true."

Feldman clears his throat. "Well now, how is it that he falls into my hands?'

"Well didn't you write a book on people like him?"

"No, not really." Feldman glances at the book displayed prominently on his shelf. "My book defrauds the so-called techniques some doctors use to treat schizophrenics. How it sounds, I am the state's last chance to help this person."

"I wouldn't know, Doctor."

Feldman sighs, "Have Max and Phil bring him up."

"Yes, Doctor."

It seems like only moments pass before the guards bring in his new patient. "That was quick, gentlemen."

"He was in a hurry to see you," Phil smiles.

Feldman looks over his new patient, a small man, but he holds himself like a giant; very generic looking, could be anyone's brother or son. His clothes hang off his frame as if they were hand-me-downs from a much larger man. His hands are cuffed, but between his hands he holds a plain cloth-bound book. As far as Feldman can tell, there is no writing on the binding or cover.

"Gentlemen, he doesn't need the handcuffs. He is no harm to me and I have nothing he could use to harm himself."

Max speaks up, "He wants it this way, Doc."

Feldman flinches.

"Doc, everything okay?" Phil asks.

Feldman shakes his head to clear it. The man looks harmless enough. What happened to the other doctors might just be coincidence.

"Yes, everything is fine." He turns toward the patient and motions to the chair in front of his desk, "Please have a seat…."

The man moves toward the desk. "Most people know me as James… James Ryan. A few know me as Cuthric Orion. It's a pleasure to meet you again."

"Well, what would you like me to call you?"

James laughs and leans across the desk, "Scary bastard."

"Now I don't think we need to call you any thing like that," Feldman glances down at the folder.

"Oh, you will Doctor, in the end. Oh, and don't worry. I won't call you Doc."

A shock passes through Feldman's body and he struggles to regain composure. "You may call me what you like. Please have a seat. Gentlemen, thank you. I won't need you any longer."

Max and Phil nod and walk out the door.

James takes a seat.

"May I ask why the handcuffs?" Feldman motions to James Ryan's cuffed hands.

"To keep myself in check... Well, myself and the others."

Feldman nods and makes some notes. "Okay. Is this were we start?"

"No, doctor. We started when you looked back out at the rain."

"Excuse me?"

"Didn't you look back at the sidewalk in that little area between doors?"

"In the foyer?"

"Yes. I guess that is what it's called."

Feldman convinces himself it was only a lucky guess and picks up a pencil. Feldman stops for a moment. Wasn't he already holding a pencil? He looks down at his notepad. It was blank. "Yes, I did look back at the rain. I enjoy the rain, for the most part. Now if you don't mind, let's get to our work at hand. How many voices do you hear?"

"In total, three. There is me, Cuthric, and the monster."

Feldman takes a deep breath. He could feel this was going to be a long day.

"Which of the three would you like to talk about?"

"None"

Feldman curls his brow, "None?"

"If I had it my way, none."

"Okay. Why don't we start with what you said earlier?"

"Which was?"

"It's a pleasure to meet you *again*. I don't recall us ever meeting."

"We have met two other times. Once about 15 years ago, but I was an older man who chained smoked. Then about a month ago, I was a weaker person, not truly formed, and in fact, neither were you."

Feldman scribbles on his notepad and reminds himself to screen state cases before he accepts them in the future. He has his hands full today. He'd better have Lisa clear his calendar. "Excuse me for a moment."

"Take your time, doctor."

Feldman walks out of his office into the waiting room. "Lisa, do I have any other patients today?"

She looks at her computer, "No, everyone has been rescheduled."

"Really?!"

"Yes, that's what you wanted. Wasn't it?"

"Yes, but I hadn't told you yet"

"Well you must have or I have the power to read minds," Lisa laughs. "Maybe I should be doing your job."

Feldman gives her a quick half smile, "I must be working too many hours."

Lisa's laugh turns to a concerned smile, "Are you sure you're alright Doctor? I can get Max and Brian back up here to take the patient away."

"Brian?"

Lisa kind of rolls her eyes. "Yes, Brian. Max's helper, been his helper for five years now."

Feldman feels his forehead crinkle and his eyes narrow, "I'm sure his name is Phil."

"Phil? No it's Brian." Lisa looks at him with genuine concern. "You sure you don't want to take the day off? Does this guy make you that jumpy? He's not like the last one the state gave you, is he? I mean, given what happened to those other doctors..."

Feldman shakes his head a bit. "No. No... I will be fine. He may be a little quirky, but I don't feel he's a danger to me."

"Alright, but if you have any problem or worries just let me know and I will call the guards."

"I will, Lisa."

Feldman walks back into his office and sees James sitting in the chair, looking at the blank pages of his book.

"It has started," James whispers.

"What has started?" Feldman asks.

"Oh, nothing." James clears his throat and closes the book. "I see your nameplate on the desk. J.R. Feldman. What does the J stand for?"

Feldman was taken aback for a moment. He hadn't displayed that plaque since the attack. "May I ask where you got that?"

"It was sitting right here by your picture." James reaches out with both cuffed hands and picks up the plaque.

Feldman didn't remember pulling it out of his desk. In fact, he didn't remember bringing it back to the office.

"So, Doctor Feldman, does the J stand for Jay, James, maybe Jack? No wait, I know. John. That's it John. Good strong name."

Feldman had to stop and think for a moment. *Was his first name John? John. Right, it is John. God, I do need to take some time off.* Feldman forces a smile and puts his hand out. "If you don't mind, could I have that back please?"

James looks down at the plaque, and sees that he is fumbling with it.

"Sure, Doctor. I didn't mean any harm," James leans forward and hands the plaque to Feldman. "I wasn't going to use it like your one patient. You remember, the one who always called you Doc."

Feldman quickly puts the plaque in his top left drawer. "Now, how do you know about that, James?"

"Well that is quite simple, Doctor. It's in the book the monster gave me."

"One of your voices gave you a book?"

"Yes, you could say that. Here. Take a look, but I do want it back." James hands him the old olive green hardbound book. The cover is made of coarsely stitched cloth smells of mold.

Feldman flips through the blanks pages. "Don't worry, James, I won't keep your book. What is it called?"

"Immortal."

103

Feldman hands the book back. "Immortal? So the monster gave you a book called Immortal. Does it outline how he is immortal?"

"Now that is a hard question to answer. I would have to say yes and then no. It is more important to the monster to make you and me immortal. That way he becomes immortal also."

Feldman points to himself and then to James. "You and I?"

"Yes, quite funny don't you think?"

Feldman sits back down in his leather chair behind his desk. He picks up his pad and pencil and makes a few notes.

James sits back in his chair and sighs, as if relieved about something.

Feldman looks up from his notepad, "That sigh makes me think that you were nervous about coming here."

"No, not really, John." James leans forward, as if to reveal a deep confidence, "Now, Cuthric hates doctors and he will do anything -- and I do mean anything -- to drive one nuts. But my big fear was that the monster might have changed the story again."

Feldman quickly makes note of that, trying not to take his eyes off his patient. "Ah, I see. I would like to come back to the monster a little later. Tell me more about Cuthric Orion."

"Well, he's the one that wants me to hurt myself all the time. He wants to test the boundaries to see if we really are immortal. That what happened to the other doctors, if you were wondering."

Feldman pulls a new notebook from his bottom right drawer, checking if the can of mace was still there. He thinks, "Now we are getting somewhere."

"So this Cuthric guides you in your self-destruction and caused the death of your other two doctors? I might be able to buy the first, but not the latter."

"Well it is all true, John. You see, Cuthric gives me the strength to commit the acts on my body. I'm too weak myself to do them without him, but overall it is the monster who decides what really happens." James lets out a laugh.

"Something funny in that, James?"

A huge grin spreads across James' face, "Yes, it just dawned on me. Don't you see, John? The monster first put Cuthric in my head so I would be crazy. Then he waited, giving Cuthric time to slowly slip into my head. But I just realized that, as far as reality goes, you, me and Cuthric are voices in *his* head"

The grin fades from James' face and scowl lines crease his forehead. "No, sorry John. He just changed the story a little."

Feldman slowly nods and scribbles notes furiously. He feels his own forehead tighten and wonders if he will need that can of mace.

"John, don't worry. You will not need that can of mace. I promise you that."

Feldman wonders if he'd spoken out loud or if he'd simply misunderstood what his patient said. He opted for the latter and tried to continue the discussion casually, "So you believe we are voices in the monster's head?"

"Yes."

Feldman makes a few more notes and thinks "By the time I get done curing James, I'll be able to write one hell of a book. Fiction, because there is no way in hell people will believe this."

"You're too late for that, John. The story is already being written."

Feldman decides to continue on as if James had said nothing. "So, is Cuthric talking to you right now?"

"Yes."

"And did he tell you to say that?" the question slips out.

"No."

Feldman makes a note to come back to the comment about the book later.

"Then what is Cuthric saying?"

James raises the pitch of his voice by an octave, "Crazy. I was crazy once. They me put in a small padded room. I died in that room. They buried me in the ground. Worms live in the ground, and I hate worms. They make me crazy. Crazy. I was crazy once." James lowers his pitch to normal, "He says it over and over again."

Feldman continues taking notes, "Do you know why he is saying that?"

"Yes, he does it so I will break down and do what he says."

Feldman nods and takes some more notes. Over his notepad, he watches James pick up the photo that is on his desk.

"What a lovely wife. Waiting to have children? If I were you, John, I wouldn't wait too long."

106

Feldman gives James a strange look. "What do you mean by that? My son is right in the picture, kneeling by my wife."

"Not in this one."

James turns the picture around and shows it to Feldman. Only his wife's face looks out from the photo. Feldman picks up his cell phone and hits his home number.

James turns the picture around and looks at it again. "I would ask her how your daughter Sara is."

Feldman looks at James, only questions in his eyes. James turns the picture back around and Feldman sees a young lady next to his wife. Feldman hangs up his cell phone and looks at James intently, "Well, let me guess. You can explain all of this."

James laughs and nods, "Yes I can. The monster likes to add family into his stories. He tells me it gives a character depth. Do you want to know about my family?"

Feldman feels in his bones that something is very much amiss. "What are you saying? That you're a character in a story?"

"No. *We* are. Now I think you're starting to understand."

"Understand what? That a voice in your head calls the shots in everyone's life?"

"No. Not everyone. Just you and I."

Feldman tries to make a note, but finds his hand is shaking too much to control the pencil.

"James, I really want to help," Feldman tries to steady his hand, "but I can't if you keep jumping around from voice to voice."

James laughs and stomps his foot and stands. "How can I make this any clearer, John? We are the voices, you and I. Voices – that's all we are. The words that flow from our voices have already been spoken in the monster's head and put down on the pages of this book." James thumps the old green book.

Feldman looks down at the book and sees, in old tarnished print, more than half rubbed off, the word *Immortal* on the front and spine of the book. Feldman frowns. He could have sworn that the book was blank.

"Don't you understand? A book makes the characters in it and the writer immortal. They make movies, plays and TV miniseries. It lives on and on. Immortal."

"James, please sit down. Let's talk rationally about this. A character in a book doesn't think, doesn't have feeling. Hell, a character in a book is not even alive."

"But we are alive, very much alive… John, how can I put this...? We are the writer's suicide note."

"What are you talking about? James, please sit."

"You're going to spill, you know."

Feldman extends his hands as if to ask, *What?*. His arm hits his coffee cup and it falls off the desk.

"Told you."

Feldman looks down at the coffee cup and cusses to himself. Luckily, it had been empty. He picks up the cup sets it back on his desk, then leans back in his chair. James is sitting very still in his chair, as if he'd never left it.

"Let me see if I have this right. We are the monster/writer's suicide note, but we are also alive. How can that be, James?"

"Like I told you, John. We live in his mind. We think, we talk, we can, if he wants us to, have feeling. The more the monster can make us real, the harder his suicide note is to find. Making him, and us, immortal. It's all laid out in the book."

Feldman notices that the book doesn't look so frail and dingy. The gold letters look newer. He knows for sure that something is up, but can't quite figure it out. "Now, James, please work with me a little. I know I'm real and I know you're real, and I know that the only person affecting my life and yours that neither one can control is GOD."

"For one moment, John... Just one moment, try to see it from my side. We are here for one purpose and one purpose only and that is to make the monster immortal. But, in turn, we are immortal."

"Alright, I will, for a moment, believe that we are in a story. Now if I prove you wrong will you drop the whole thing?"

"Of course, John."

Feldman steadies his hand and takes a drink of his coffee. He looks down into the nearly full cup and remembers knocking it over just moments before. Did he pour himself another cup? This patient is making him crazy. Best-selling author goes crazy....He looks at his book standing proudly on the shelf. Then slowly, it begins to dawn on him. "Wait. Wait just a moment; I'm starting to understand."

"Well that's good, John."

Feldman smiles and chuckles, "James this will not work."

"What is that, John?"

"Who put you up to this?"

"What do you mean John?"

"This… All of this… It's some type of joke.. Right? You were sent here by my colleagues to make fun of my findings. You're that street performer I saw the other day doing all of those tricks."

"No John. There was no street performer the other day, because there was no other day."

"Okay, then how did my son break this arm six weeks ago?"

"You mean your daughter."

"No, I mean my son. Just because you can change things on whim...just sleight of hand…"

"It's not me who can change things."

"Right. It's the monster."

"Precisely."

"We were born. Right?"

"You can say that."

"Being alive means that we have a beginning, middle and an end."

"Just like a book.. huh John?"

"I simple terms, I guess. But, the point is, we live. We are very complex creatures."

"John, we only become as complex as he makes us."

"I will not be drawn into your world, James." Feldman looks at the so-called patient. "I'm trying to bring you back to this world."

"That is what I am trying to explain to you. They are one and the same."

"One and the same?! "

"Yes. We are in a world of our own."

"Let's try this from a different angle. You have attempted suicide 43 times."

"No, I was successful 43 times. It was the monster who wouldn't let me die."

"See, James that is where you are wrong. You and only you made those attempts."

"No, it was Cuthric who put the ideas into my head."

"So it was Cuthric who made you try to commit suicide?"

"Yes, but as I told you, I was successful."

"Right"

There is a long silence.

Feldman feels himself becoming angry. His fingers drum the top of his desk.

"Problem, John?"

"What? No." Feldman wonders why he is angry at the small man. "Is there a chance that Cuthric would come out and speak with me?"

"Sorry, he is only allowed to speak with me. He speaks in a language only I can understand."

"Really?" Feldman makes some more notes. "Is he speaking to you right now?"

"He always speaks to me."

"What is he telling you now?"

"He's telling me that I should get up and get out of here and try to do myself in again."

"I thought that was impossible."

"That what I'm saying. From what I have read of the story, it was just going to be about a mad man and his problems, but then it grew and the monster awakened."

Feldman takes some more notes, then he stops and looks over them and notices how he has let this conversation run all over the place. He needs to get it back in control. Feldman snaps his eyes up and looked as James for a long moment.

James raises his eyebrows, "Yes doctor?"

"Well, James. This all had to start somewhere. According to your file, you seemed to have had a normal childhood, good parents, lots of friends."

"If you say so, Doctor. I'll trust what your file says. It's all just background that won't actually make it into the story anyway. Pre-writing, he calls it."

"Is there a different story you would like to tell?"

"No, I like that one."

Feldman makes some more notes. He pauses for a moment before he speaks. "See James, it's all in black and white. Your history… Your life from the beginning until now."

"No doctor, that is what the monster wants you to believe. The real truth is in this book."

"Alright, James. You seem to want to focus on the book. Let's talk about it."

James smiles "Good, doctor. Now we can get somewhere."

"Ok, how did you get the book? And were Cuthric and the monster already there in your mind?"

James laughs, "They have always been with me and you have too. But I think I understand what you mean. Cuthric has always been in my head, but he was like background noise. I could get rid of him by having a drink or two. And, like you said, my family and friends would also help me out. I had never thought of doing myself in until the book arrived."

Feldman stops writing and looks up at James. He takes a quick glance at the clock on the wall. Only ten minutes had passed since James had arrived. "Then you read the book and 'BANG' Cuthric is alive and well, along with the monster." Feldman is surprised at his own sarcastic tone.

"No, it wasn't like that at all, Doctor. It was this old green book with blank pages in it and no title. It arrived in the mail one day, wrapped in plain brown paper with no return address. Come to think of it all it the brown paper said on it was, 'Immortal'"

Feldman takes some more notes, still shaky, but feeling the conversation was finally going down the right path.

"I thought it was a joke and just dismissed it. Then the voices started. It began with the monster. He wasn't talking to me or at me. He was talking about me, as if I was just a thing, a small idea. He spoke of his first story about me and how it wouldn't fit in the bones of the woods."

"Bones of the woods?"

"I'm not real clear on that one myself."

Feldman feels that he should know that name – that it is familiar somehow. He writes it boldly in his notes.

113

James continues, "It was right after that, I believe that next morning, for whatever reason, I looked at the old green book. This time it had lettering on it. I went and looked, and there, in faded letters was 'Immortal'."

"Now, see James, we must be real. You spoke of friends, going out drinking, and mail. All before you ever got the book."

James sits in silence.

"Well, James?"

James face relaxes, "It fits the story, Doc."

Feldman feels a flash of warmth across his face. He snaps at James, "Don't call me that!" Feldman struggles to regain his composure. He speaks precisely, as if to a child. "James, you can call me John, Doctor, or Doctor Feldman. Just please don't call me Doc."

"Sorry Doc...*tor*. Anyway, the monster started talking to me as if I was someone, but he would never hear my replies. He would think, 'Of course you can't answer. You're only a character'." There was a lot of excitement in James' voice. He stared at the ceiling, and as he talked, he thumped on the book, as if to punctuate his thoughts. Each thump was a little harder. "One night I was sitting in my bed unable to sleep and I didn't know why because usually I sleep fine. Then I noticed that the green book was lying next to me. It looked brand new. I casually picked it and opened it. There were words on the page. I started to read it and must have fallen asleep. When I woke up -- if I can call it that now -- I heard 'Hello James, welcome to my nightmare.' I said 'What good does it do if I try and answer and you don't hear me?' The monster replied, 'Oh I hear you, James, nice and clear. I can feel you, your feelings. Everything. You are alive in my head. I want you to finish

114

the book and you will know where to go from there." Thump. James' fist crashes down against the book's cover.

Feldman is now worried that he may have pushed too far. "James, would you like to take a break now?"

James stops thumping and looks Feldman in the eye, a devilish grin spreading across his face as he speaks. "Oh No. no..NO, DOC.. We are just getting to the good part of the story."

"James, I really believe that we should take a small break. We've been at this for a bit."

Feldman reaches for his coffee with one hand and a secret button with the other hand.

"Careful, Doc. How you're shaking, you might spill your coffee."

As Feldman picks up his coffee cup, he sees the cup quiver and feels coffee sloshing over its sides. He pushes the button again.

"Button not working, Doc? I could have told you that. Story device. Keeps the reader tense."

Now beyond worried, Feldman concentrates on keeping James calm.

"Why do we need a break, Doc? We have only been talking for ten minutes."

Feldman glances at the clock, the time hasn't changed since the last time he looked. He looks at this watch, which reads the same as the clock on the wall.

"That's right, Doc. Time has stopped."

Feldman's nerves go raw, "James, please don't call me Doc." He stands up behind his desk.

115

"A little unnerved DOC?"

"I don't know how you are doing all of this, but it is time you quit."

"I'm not doing it Doc. I swear."

Feldman shakes his fist at his patient, "You will tell me what is going on, and you will stop playing these games."

James opens his book and sets it on the desk. Feldman eyes widen, there are words on the pages now.

"See... You do see it now.... You see the words."

Feldman shakes his head, "No."

"Yes, Doc, words. Making us immortal... Making us the keepers of the note."

Feldman shakes his head again, "NO!"

"And as we speak, you're fumbling for that gun in the top drawer."

Feldman looks down and sees the top left drawer is open. Sitting on top of the sharpened pencils is a pearl handled pistol. Feldman looks back up at James. James grins.

"What does the note say, James?" Feldman asks coldly.

"I don't know. The monster wouldn't tell me."

"Where is this note, James?"

"I don't know, Doc. If we think this out, we might be able to change things."

"Oh I plan too, James. I plan too."

"DOC PLEASE NO...." James screams.

Feldman hears the echo of the gun being fired. He watches James and the leather chair flip over in slow

116

motion, sees James body collapse into a heap. James lets out a moan. Feldman's eyes widen as rushes over to his patient.

"Oh god, John. This is not the way I wanted it to end, forever lying in a pool of my own blood, never to die, just lying here, forever dying."

Feldman lets the weapon drop from his hand and covers his face. He doesn't notice the smoking end of his nameplate as it bounces onto the floor. In a muffled voice, he cries, "This isn't real -- it can't be real. I am not the sort of man to do that. God, please let this not be real...Please don't let me be immortal."

In the Air Tonight

by John E. Miller

"Robbie...Robbie! Wake up. It's getting ready to launch!"

As Robert opened his eyes, he saw his Aunt Sally standing in the doorway to his room, wearing what he called her Betty Crocker dress. He knew about Betty Crocker from the plaque his great-great grandmother won in a cook-off contest. The plaque still hung proudly next to the kitchen stove. The woman on the plaque wore a dress that had under skirting and pleats. Robert laughed to himself; it's 2112 and his Aunt Sally is wearing a light yellow dress that looks like it came from the 1950's.

The kids at school teased him about his aunt, but he didn't care. He loves his aunt and uncle and he believes in what they do. His aunt was waking Robert up to watch the shuttle take off with it greatest cargo -- the strays and unwanted animals that were being sent to good homes on the colonized planets. Robert, his Uncle Sam, and his Aunt Sally had been collecting money for this mission. Robert felt that it was a win-win situation. The animals got to live and the people elsewhere got to have pets.

"Come on, sleepy head! You're going to miss it," his Aunt leaned over to kiss his forehead.

He waved her away. He loved his Aunt, but at 14 he was too old to have her kissing him.

Robert rolled out of bed, not bothering to change out of his nightclothes, and plopped onto the couch between his Uncle Sam and Hamlet, their big, clumsy mutt. The 39" flat screen was already on. It didn't bother Robert that he had to stay with his aunt and uncle. His mother and father were in the Space Navy. He could not go with them on their tour of duty because it was not permitted for officers' children to travel on the tours. As they watched the launch, Robert could not help but think of one day when he would be on a shuttle heading to see his parents.

***

A few mornings later, Robert checked his e-mail to see if his parents had written to him. To his surprise, he had two new messages. He looked at the names. One was from his only true friend Timmy and the other was from a person named Mary. A thought flashed in Robert's mind, "Spam or a virus…Naw that had been outlawed for 100 years..."

He laughed to himself about how the old stories that his grandfather had told him came to mind like that. His aunt and uncle would tell him that they were just spooky stories and weren't real. He clicked on the e-mail from this person named Mary.

Dear Robert Crystal,

Thank you for sending me a cat. It helps make thing livable on this new planet. It's called Mobius 9. It has two moons, but the air is breathable and plants seem to like the ground here.

I named the cat 'Robert'. He's a Tom cat, all black with a white spot on top of his head. Maybe if you get time you could write to me.

Friend (I hope),
Mary Carver

Robert thought for a moment, "Why not? This way I'll get to know more about the Tom cat and maybe have a new friend". He clicked the Reply button.

Dear Mary Carver,

Sure, I would like to be friends. I can tell you about what is happening on Earth and you can tell me what is happening in space... Well, on the new colony Mobius 9.

Thank you for naming the Tom cat after me, but you didn't have to. How is he doing?

I'm going out today to try and raise money so we can send more animal to you guys.

I have some more e-mails to check, but I will write more later.

Friends (Forever I hope)

Robert Crystal

p.s. You can call me Rob.

Robert hit send and smiled. He sat in a dreamlike state for a moment wondering what Mary and the Tom cat looked like. Then he remembered the other letter from Timmy and opened it. To his surprise, it was an invitation to a birthday party at the pizza arcade place. Robert had eaten pizza from there before, but he was never allowed to go there because his aunt and uncle thought video games were a waste of time. Robert could understand that it was more important to save the animals than to play some dumb game, but it would be nice to go to Timmy's party. Robert decided he'd ask if he could go.

Robert walked into the kitchen and saw his aunt and uncle making animal treats. "Ummm, Sally, Sam, can I go to a birthday party?"

They smiled.

His aunt looked up from the dough she was mixing, "We got the e-mail also. I don't see why not, as long as you don't play those games."

"I would never do that," Robert promised.

"Alright then, you can go. Now why don't you e-mail Timmy back and let him know it's okay. We have to leave soon for the pound."

"Alright." As Robert ran to his room, he could hear his uncle and aunt laugh. Robert could hardly wait until Saturday and the party. On the way to and from the pound, that was all Robert could talk about. His uncle and aunt just listened to him rattling on and smiled.

***

A few nights later, Robert finished his homework and checked his e-mail. He had one from his parents and one from Mary. After reading and replying to his parents' letter he opened Mary's.

Dear Rob,

I got your last letter I'm glad that you get to go to the party. You'll have to let me know how it went. It was a strange day today. Some new space cruisers went by. Robert (Tom cat) and I got a bad feeling about them.

Mom said that the news said it was nothing to worry about.

Anyway, they got the school built, so I will be starting tomorrow.

I need to get ready for bed.

Friends forever,
Miss you,

Mary

p.s. Here's the picture I promised you.

    Robert opened the attached file. It was a picture of Mary and her Tom cat with the two moons in the background. He smiled and ran his finger over her face on the screen "I wonder if she would be my girlfriend."

    He clicked the Reply button.

Dear Mary,

I love the picture. You didn't say anything about the ones I sent you.

Yeah I can't wait until the party I have never been to one.

I got teased about my aunt at school again, and this one kid wanted to fight me, but I was taught not to. I have a black eye now, and Timmy beat up the bully for me.

Anyway, I have a question to ask you, but not yet.

Friends forever,

Rob

p.s. You're kind of cute and I like Robert. He's so big and fluffy.

***

Robert couldn't believe it was Saturday and he was on his way to the party. His uncle had given him light rail money. He had never ridden on it without them. It was fun and scary at the same time.

When Robert got to his stop, he ran down to the pizza place. Most of the guests were already there.

"Where do I put your present?" he asked Timmy.

"On that table over there. Get some pizza while you're at it."

"Okay."

Robert looked at all the presents Timmy was getting. His seemed small compared to the other ones, but he knew it was the thought that counts. He smiled to himself because he and Mary had talked about what to get him. He grabbed some pizza and went to talk to Timmy, who was standing by a game console.

"Look, Robert." Timmy's voice cracked with excitement. "It's a new video game."

"So?"

"You don't play video games?"

"No!"

"Don't you have a game console or PC games?"

"No?? Should I?"

"Come on, let's play."

"Naw my aunt and uncle said I can't."

"Aw come on. They won't know."

Robert looked at the video table. "Space Wars" was painted on the side and above it, "New 3D action". Robert looked at all the buttons, then looked at his friend's anxious face. "I don't know."

"Come on, it's my birthday."

Robert thought a little more. "I don't have any money."

"That's okay. All the games are free for us today. My mom and dad rented out the whole place for me."

Robert thought of his own parents. One day when they got home, they would do stuff like that too. He smiled at his friend, "I guess one game won't hurt. What do we do?"

"We get the controls of the Space Navy."

"Really?" Robert raised his eyebrows in surprise.

Timmy laughed, "Not for real, silly. It's just a game."

"Oh," Robert felt embarrassed and a little let down.

Timmy pointed to the instructions printed on the side. "It's fun anyway. Look, there are three modes. In the first, you play the computer. Second, one of us plays the alien and the other plays the Navy. And in the third mode, we both play as the Space Navy and the computer plays the alien."

Robert shrugged, "Which one do you want to play? It's your birthday."

"I want to be the alien. You can play the Navy." He moved around to the other side of the game table.

"Okay…" Robert eyed the controls hesitantly. It looked harmless enough.

Timmy pushed the button to start play. The machine came alive and, floating above it, a holographic image of 3D ships hovered at the opposing sides of the table.

"Wow, it's so real!" Timmy gasped.

"Huh?"

"The last version was on the screen with 3D graphics. But now you can see it from all angles."

Robert looked at the holographics. He eyed his enemy and starting pressing the controls. As his navy defeated one ship after another, he felt something stir in his heart. They played three games together, and each time Robert won by a higher number of points.

"Ok, I thought you said that you didn't play games," Timmy scowled.

"I don't."

"Wow, you're a natural at it!" Timmy eyed his friend, appreciatively. "You should play against the computer. Each level gets harder and you get more controls."

"Really?" Robert felt his excitement grow.

"I've got to play with some of the other guests. I'll be back later if you want to play some more."

"Okay," Robert said distractedly, looking at the controls that had been disabled when he played his friend. He pushed single player and started playing. He rose in rank, commanding more and more ships, gaining more controls, fighting more powerful aliens. Robert didn't know how long he had played, but when he finally lost, he held high score.

"Young man?"

Robert jumped with a start and saw that a large man stood beside him.

"Were you with the birthday party?"

"Yes?!"

"Ah, well here you go... I'm about ready to close."

He handed Robert a white box and a note, then walked off. Robert opened the note and read it.

Bobby,
I'm sorry I left without saying goodbye. But you were having so much fun, I didn't want to bother you. Thanks for the present. It was the best. See you at school.

Your friend,
Timmy

"Crap, I need to get home!' Robert felt guilty and worried about what punishment might await him. Not that his aunt and uncle would be unfair....he had just never disobeyed them like this before. He raced back to the light rail and hardly noticed the world racing by as it sped him toward his home and his punishment. When he reached his stop, he ran to his house. He opened the door just as he saw his aunt reach for the phone.

"I'm home," he yelled.

"Thank God!" she ran over and kissed his forehead. "I was starting to worry. How was the party?"

"Great. Here I brought you some cake home."

"Why, thank you," his aunt took the white box from him and put it in the refrigerator. "I guess you're not hungry?"

"I'm starved."

His aunt gave him a strange look, "Didn't you eat the pizza?"

"Ummmm, some," Robert stuttered, then grinned. "I just prefer your cooking."

His aunt laughed and ran her fingers through his hair, "Well, I wish you would tell me these things."

"I'm going to write Mary real quick." Robert scurried out from under his aunt's hand and down the hall to his room.

"Oh okay. Dinner will be soon."

"Okay."

Robert ducked into his room and woke up his computer. He went right to his e-mail, and saw a letter waiting for him from Mary. Robert clicked on it.

Dear Rob,

I don't think that's our ships. I'm a little scared and so is Robert. They called off school early for no reason.

I did love your pictures and you're cute too.

What was your question?

Love,

Mary

"Love… she said love," Robert looked at the picture of Mary he'd printed and tacked to his wall. "I wonder if she knows what I'm going to ask."

Robert bent over his keyboard, smiling, and clicked Reply.

Dear Mary,

I had a great time at the party. I found a new game. I don't usually play games, but this one was really cool.

Actually, I never have played a game, but this one is different.

I'm at the command of the Space Navy!

I still have a question for you.

Love always,

Rob

Robert sat in front in his screen…. "Love? Well, she said it first." He clicked Send.

Robert put on his PJs and laid on his bed thinking about the game until his aunt called him to dinner.

***

Robert found himself sitting on the light rail again, as he had every school day for the second week in a row, heading to the pizza place after school. Once again, he'd skipped his lunch to save his money for the light rail and the game. He had called Aunt Sally earlier, telling her that he was with Timmy. It wasn't a full lie; Timmy was going to meet him there.

"I can't believe I'm going back to that game…. I'll make it up to Sally and Sam."

The pizza place's owner Will was standing by the machine when Robert ran in.

He smiled, "Guess what?"

Robert groaned, "It's broke, isn't it?"

"No. Try again."

"Hmmmmm, I don't know."

"New upgrade," Will pointed to the Space Navy game table. "It seems that you maxed out the game, so I had to get the upgrade. Oh, and I thought you might like this." Will handed him a rolled up plastic board. "I got it as a free promo for the upgrade."

Robert unrolled it and grinned. It was a map of the known inhabited worlds. "Thanks." He motioned to the game table, "Is it ready?"

"Yes, but one more thing."

"What's that?"

"There is a contest."

"Really?"

"Yep," Will unrolled the poster for Robert to read.

Calling all Space Navy warriors
The Navy needs you!

1st place – 1 million credits and a full scholarship to Naval Academy
2nd place – Get a Space Navy Machine of your very own with lifetime free upgrades
3rd place – 100,000 dollars
Only one entry per arcade

Robert's eyes widened.

"And guess who I chose."

"I don't know. Timmy?"

Will smiled, "You, silly."

"I don't think so…." Robert heard his uncle's unmistakable voice. He turned and saw his Uncle Sam standing at the door of the arcade, frowning. Robert's face turned red and he couldn't meet his uncle's eyes. He stared at the floor.

"I think you should go out to the car and wait for me, young man. Your aunt is waiting for you in the car."

"Now, wait a minute…." Will turned toward his uncle.

Robert walked slowly out to the car. He felt bad about leaving Will alone with his uncle, but he figured he had it worse. He had to face his Aunt Sally. Right before he reached the car, he felt a hand fall on his shoulders. He looked up and saw his Uncle Sam with a smile on his face.

"Will explained everything to me. When we get home, we will talk about it. Robert, you shouldn't hide things from us. We love you and worry about you."

"I know. I'm sorry."

Sam's smile broadened, "Come on, get in the car. But not a word about it to your aunt until we get home. You and I will explain it to her over dinner."

When they got home, Sally made dinner while Robert sat quietly at the kitchen table, trying to do his homework. All he could think about was the contest.

At last dinner was ready. As his uncle had promised, they talked over the contest and how Will had been working with Robert so he could win the prize. Sally was dead against it. Finally, Sam gave up trying and told her that they would talk about it after dinner. Robert's heart sank past his stomach. He finished his dinner, but went to his room without dessert. Disheartened, he checked his e-mail. No message from his parents, but there was one from Mary. His heart leapt a little as he opened it.

Dear Rob,

I could not wait to tell you, but you have to keep it quiet. There are other races out here.... NO JOKE!

I have a question for you...Ummm... I know we are worlds apart. But I think you're kind of cute and was wondering if we... well... if we could be VERY close friends.

If you don't want to, I understand...☹

I hope you do. ☺

Love (I think I mean it)

Mary

"VERY close friends...Love (I think I mean it)..." Robert read over her letter again and again, his smile got bigger each time he read the words, "You're darn right"

"Robert?"

Robert quickly closed his e-mail. He didn't feel it was the time to let his aunt and uncle know he had a girlfriend. Not yet."

"Yes, Aunt Sally?"

"Your uncle and I talked it over and it would be nice if you won. BUT I want you to understand that it is just a game and if you lose, you just lost. You're not a loser."

Robert kept his smile to himself.

Sally let out a sigh, "Robert you are listening?"

"Yes ma'am."

"Robert, I still don't know."

"Aunt Sally... please. It's only a game. And if I do win, my college will be paid for."

She shook her head and lowered it. "Don't get caught up in it."

"I won't," Robert smiled and kissed his aunt's cheek. "I love you."

Sally smiled a sad smile and walked out of the room. Robert turned back to his computer so he could reply to Mary. This was the best day of his life. A girlfriend, life on other planets, AND he gets to play in the contest.

Dear Mary,

Wow, life on other planets that isn't us... Cool!

Guess what... I get to be in a contest playing Space Navy... Isn't that cool?

And about being very special friends, that was my question also. ☺

Love,

Your special friend,

Rob

***

Every afternoon Robert went to the pizza place to play Space Navy. Every evening, after he did his homework, he marked the location of each battle on his map and e-mailed Mary.

At last, the day of the first round of the competition arrived. Robert got to the pizza place early and surveyed the crowd. Timmy was there, along with other people he recognized from school. Newspaper and television reporters were there too. He recognized one of them as a reporter who'd covered the launch of pets to Mobius 9. He smiled at the reporter, proudly pointing to the t-shirt Will had given him with the name and address of the pizza parlor and Robert's name on the back.

The first competitor to go up against Robert was one of the older bullies from school. He wore a t-shirt with the name of an arcade across town. "Here is my chance to get even," Robert thought.

"Everyone, please listen up," a man's voice boomed out from the speakers, a little too loud, but it silenced the crowd. "Today's event is called "Usher". It is a land-based battle and will be single elimination. Players, your controls are set to tournament rules. May the best person win!"

Robert smiled and looked over at his aunt. She looked worried and sad. Robert mouthed, "Don't worry, I have this one in the bag."

She and his uncle nodded, "Remember, it's only a game." she mouthed back.

Robert just smiled and took his place in front of the controls.

It didn't take Robert long to beat the bully. And, like all bullies, he was a poor loser, claiming that his controls were rigged and there was no way a shrimp like Robert could

133

beat him. The judges examined the game table and shook their heads. The bully threatened them with his fist and cursed. "Poor loser," Will whispered over his shoulder.

Robert smiled at Will, "He always has been."

"You did good," Will said.

"I'll do even better next game," Robert grinned, his nervousness replaced by a confidence he'd never known he had. He took his place in front of his next opponent and waited for the judge to signal them to start.

Robert was surprised how easy it was to beat the other players. His combat losses were very minimal. Finally, he reached the last round and faced an older man with short dark hair, wearing nicely pressed clothes. No arcade t-shirt, just a blue button-down with an insignia Robert didn't recognize. "Where are you from?" Robert mouthed. The man just smiled and nodded.

Robert took his place at the controls. The judge approached the table and addressed Robert and his opponent more than he did the crowd. "Alright, gentlemen. You are the last two. Whoever wins this will go to the next level of the contest…. Good luck."

It was the longest game Robert had ever played in his life, but in the end, he won. While his losses of men to aliens were higher than usual, he felt good about it. When it ended, his opponent walked up and shook Robert's hand, "You're very good. I've never seen a person win with such minimal loss of men before."

"Thank you," Robert replied.

Will walked up, "Everyone, I would like to be the second person to shake the winner's hand." He shook Robert's hand and then handed him a trophy, three tickets to Moon Base 1 and a check for $1,000. He leaned over and whispered, "I knew you were my best choice."

Robert was more impressed with the tickets than anything else. Finally, he would get to go to space.

Robert was so excited when the got home that he rushed to his room and marked off where he had battled on the map. He planned to do this for every win he had. Sally made a place on the shelf in the living room for his trophy, Robert stared at it for a long time, then he noticed a plaque on the shelf. He looked at it closely. He had seen the plaque before, and always thought that it was his dad's for graduating from the Naval Academy. But now he noticed it had a different name on it, "Mark T. Bencher."

Robert heard the television turn on. He noticed his uncle had come into the room. He decided to ask about the plaque. "Uncle Sam,… Who is Mark T. Bencher?"

His uncle started, then walked up to Robert. He put his arm around his nephew and guided him toward the couch, "You'd better sit for this one."

Robert looked at his uncle, confused. But he sat down on the couch, as asked.

His uncle spoke in a low voice, "Mark Bencher is Sally's brother. He was in the top 10 of his graduating class."

"Why haven't I ever met him? Is he a great commander in the Navy?"

"Well…. I guess you're old enough to know. You see, Mark liked to play online games and at the time Space Navy could only be played online. Everything was okay for the first 3 months, but then he started playing every night after he got home from work, then he started playing all night and stopped going to work. The game had taken over his life. It broke your aunt's heart when she had to put him in a home. The doctors had to give her medicine for her nerves."

"So that is why she doesn't like me playing the game." Now Robert understood his aunt's reluctance and he even felt kind of bad for pushing the issue of the contest.

"Yep," his uncle shook his head sadly. "Too bad, too. The kid had promise."

"I swear I will never get that bad!" Robert was earnest in his promise.

"I know, champ. I just have to keep reminding *her* of that."

Robert sat for a few moments, watching television with his uncle. Then he remembered he hadn't told Mary about winning the contest. "Oh, I need to write Mary about today!" He jumped from the couch.

His uncle laughed and smiled, "You'd better go do that! Girlfriends like to be told about stuff like that."

Robert was in his room before he realized what his uncle had said. "He knows...," Robert started to head back to find out whether he'd said anything to Aunt Sally, but decided he didn't really want to know. He woke up his computer and checked his e-mails. As he'd hoped, there was a message from Mary.

Dear Rob,

I got some more pictures of Robert and me (and you know what). We can't talk about them anymore.

Anyway, school is going well. I haven't made many friends, but that's OK. I still have you right?

Love always,

Mary

Robert opened the pictures. He saw a strange ship not too far from where Mary was standing with Robert the cat. So that's what they really looked like. Robert clicked Reply.

Dear Mary,

Thank you for the pictures of you and Robert the cat. I see what you mean.

Guess what? I won and now I get to go to space... Well to the moon at least. That's a start. I can't wait!

Of course you still have me!

Love always,

Rob

On his star map Robert encircled Mobius 9 with a heart.

***

Robert was afraid that the three weeks between tournaments would drag on forever, but luckily, writing to Mary and his newfound popularity at school made time pass quickly.

The day before the tournament finally arrived. Timmy accompanied them to the launch. His uncle gave Timmy the keys to the house. Timmy would be watching Hamlet while they were gone. Timmy patted Robert on the back and wished him luck.

Robert, his uncle, and his aunt stepped on the shuttlecraft destined for the moon. Robert was bummed that he would not get to write to Mary while he was on the moon and, he had to admit, he was a little nervous about the tournament.

The ship thrust as it took off, sending a thrill through Robert's insides. He was going to space. He watched out the window, as Earth grew smaller and smaller.

"Welcome to first class," a voice interrupted his thoughts. "My name is Wendy and I will be your server. May I get you something?"

"Two glasses of white wine," his uncle answered. "And he will have a cream soda."

Wendy smiled and walked off.

"Wow, first class!" Robert exclaimed.

"Oh that's not all," his aunt actually seemed excited. "They have set us up in a major hotel and yes..." Robert's aunt smiled at him, her eyes twinkling teasingly, "it has Internet access."

The young lady came back with their drinks. As she leaned over to put Robert's drink on his tray, she whispered, "So you're one of the winners of the Space Navy contest?"

"Yes," his aunt answered proudly, "he is our nephew Robert."

"Well, hello, Robert. You see all of these people in first class with you?"

Robert nodded.

"They also won. I guess you will be playing most of them."

Robert looked around the room at his opponents. A few of them were kids about his age, but most of them were older. He lifted his soda and sipped.

"Good luck," Wendy said. "Let me know if you need anything else."

"Thanks," Robert felt his nervousness return. "I'll need it."

They watched some on flight movies. The last one ended just before landing, but Robert hardly knew what the movies were about. He was in space and tomorrow he would be up against all these other people in the tournament.

The ship landed without any problems and they walked through the docking tunnel to the terminal gateway, where a tall young lady waited. She informed them that while in the hotel everything was on the house for the whole weekend, win or lose. She led them through the terminal and out onto the moon base street. Robert looked through the transparent dome at the night sky. Earth hung like a blue and white moon overhead. "Funny how it looks so different up here," he thought, as he moved with the rest of the contestants down the street toward the hotel. When they stepped inside the hotel, it was like stepping into a jungle. Plants grew everywhere and people stared at them from small tables nestled between the tropical trees.

"Let's go to the room first," his uncle said. "Then we'll come down and get some dinner."

Robert turned on the computer as soon as he got to his room. He checked his e-mail, but there was no message from Mary. He figured as much. She thought he wouldn't have Internet access. He decided to drop her a line.

Dear Mary,

By the time you get this and write me back it should be almost time for me to leave for the tournament. Most of the people I'll be battling tomorrow are older than me.

Wish me luck!

Love,

Your boyfriend, Robert

p.s. I can see Earth from here and it looks like a moon.

After eating a large dinner, Robert rested for the evening. He didn't want to be tired for the tournament. In the morning, Robert woke up and showered quickly. After he was dressed, he went into the suite's shared room where breakfast was waiting. His uncle had ordered his favorite, a ham and cheese omelet. He took his plate and woke up the computer to check his e-mail. As he'd hoped, there was a message from Mary waiting. He clicked it.

Dear Rob,

I hope you do well.

Big Hug and a Kiss,
Love,

Mary

That seemed short and the point. He shrugged and turned away from the computer. Maybe she had something to do today. He wouldn't let it bother him.

When they got to the room where the tournament was to be held, Robert saw a large wall hanging announcing that the tournament would be televised.

Robert took his seat in the waiting area. The announcer leaned over the mic, "Welcome, everyone, to Round 2 of the first annual and, may I add, televised Space Navy tournament."

A round of claps and hoots. The announcer smiled and waited for the noise to die down. "This is the second round of the tournament. It is being held on three colonized planets and the Earth's moon. Today's game is called 'Search and Destroy' and it is a single-elimination battle. After today's tournament, the four finalists from this competition will go on to the next location, where they will battle the other twelve finalists who will be chosen on the three colonial planets. Where are they going? That's our secret."

People hooted and clapped their hands. Again, he stood silent as the crowd quieted down.

"The four finalists will receive 30,000 dollars, a full expense paid trip to the next round, which will take place on Jupiter's moon, Io.

More clapping and hooting

"So, without further delay, players find your seats."

Robert looked at the number he had been given and found the seat that matched it. Across from him was a heavyset woman around his aunt's age. He smiled at her and she smiled back. When the whistle sounded, they both took the defensive. Finally, the woman gave in and her fleet charged toward his. He fired mercilessly, watching one by one as her spacecraft burst into flames. As her last plane went down, he thought he saw tears moisten the corners of her eyes. She wiped them away quickly and smiled, "Good match."

"You too," Robert said graciously. "You made me work for it."

She smiled at him, "You're about my son's age. You'd like him. He plays Space Navy too, but not like you do. He hasn't learned the importance of staying alive."

Robert grinned, "Yeah....I'm pretty particular about keeping my guys alive. Maybe because my parents are in the real Space Navy."

She patted his arm, "They must be proud of you."

Robert shrugged, "Yeah, I guess." He almost told her that he hadn't heard from them in over two weeks, but didn't.

She went to sit next to her two kids to watch the rest of the contest. Robert waited to be assigned his next opponent.

It was a very long day for Robert, but each round he found himself fighting better. And each round he won graciously. Once again, it was the last match that gave him trouble. His opponent was a man who seemed to be in his 40s. His head was shaved and he wore a tan button down shirt and dark blue slacks. The last match was set to a different adventure and was much more complex. They had also added sound effects and he could hear the bantering of the pilots and officers, making it all seem more real. He imagined his father and mother were among them. His opponent fired on him and one of his ships swerved, taking damage in its rear. Repairable, but he would need to concentrate. He tuned out the background chatter and focused on the game. By the skin of his teeth, he won.

Robert's opponent walked up to him and looked at the score. "Wow! You are good. Only a 7% loss of men. I have never seen anyone to do that well." He smiled and shook Robert's hand. Robert felt the man's ring press against his hand. He shook the man's hand, hardly able to believe that he had won.

"The best man really did win," the older man said, as he rubbed Roberts head.

The judge handed him a medal and a plaque. "Your tickets and money will be hand-delivered when you get home," the judge whispered, but Robert hardly heard what he said, as the audience's applause surrounded him. He was number one.

That evening, there was a huge party to honor Robert and the other three finalists. By the time the party ended, Robert was too tired to check his e-mail. He would be sure to write to Mary in the morning.

***

Robert barely slept that night. In his mind, he went over each of his battles, the commands he'd given, and the damage they'd done. In the morning, he woke up the computer and checked his e-mail. Nothing.

Mary,

Can you believe it? I won! I'm in the semifinals. I got a medal and another trophy and $30,000.

I still can't believe it… it must have been your luck and kiss that helped me.

Love always,

Rob

Robert didn't watch the movies on the way home. Instead, he looked out in space and dreamed about the days he'd travel to distant stars as a real Space Navy commander. As they approached Earth, he watched the ship's reentry.

By the time they got home and ate dinner, Robert was quite tired. In fact, he fell asleep at the dinner table. His uncle led him to bed. Robert woke up a little and listened to his uncle and aunt talking in their room down the hall.

"I don't know about this, Sam." his aunt said.

"What, love?"

"I think it's too much for him. He's exhausted."

"He knows what he's doing, Sally."

"Yes, but I can't do it again."

"This is different, Sally. Believe me."

"I worry."

"I don't."

Robert heard his door open and felt soft warm lips kiss his forehead. He rolled over and fell back to sleep.

In the morning, he awoke to the smell of breakfast cooking. Bacon, home fries, eggs, and toast. He scrambled out of bed. Having slept through dinner, he was starved. However, there was one thing he had to do before eating. He woke up his computer and checked his e-mail. There was one from Mary at last. He opened it.

Rob,

I'm so happy for you. I wish I could have been there for you, with a real hug and kiss. I've been telling my mom and dad about you and how well you're doing in the tournament. I would tell my friends at school, but I really don't have any.

Love always,

Mary

Robert would write to her that evening. Right now he wanted food, plus he had to get ready for school. He raced to the kitchen and gobbled down a plate of bacon, three eggs, potatoes, and toast. Then he hurried to get ready for school.

As Robert was taking a shower, he thought he heard the doorbell ring. He turned off the water and dried himself. As he dressed, he could hear soft voices, two men and a woman.

Then he heard his Aunt Sally say in a loud voice, not screaming, but firm. "No! I will not have anything to do with it!"

He heard her stomp into the kitchen. Robert knew it had to be something with the game.

He stepped out into the hallway and could see his uncle talking to an older man, "Yes, he will be there."

Robert could tell that his uncle was a little nervous. And the older man seemed familiar to him. He figured the man must have something to do with the contest. The man handed Robert's uncle an envelope. His uncle walked the man to the door and escorted him outside. As his uncle stepped back in, he saw Robert. He smiled and winked. His uncle walked over to him and whispered, "Here are our tickets and a check for the money you won. But right now, I need to speak with your aunt. Why don't you go play outside or on your computer?"

Robert nodded and headed for his room. He heard his aunt and uncle arguing and he knew it was about him and the contest. To Robert, it seemed that they argued forever. Then it finally got quiet. He heard footsteps and a light knock at his door.

"Robert, can I come in?"

He could tell by his aunt's voice she had been crying.

"Sure. You're always welcome to come in my room."

His aunt walked in. He noticed her eyes were red and puffy.

"I won't keep you long," she said softly. "Your uncle is getting ready to take you to school. I just have one question for you."

"Shoot."

She gave him a weak smile. "Are you sure you want to keep going in this contest? You know it is only going to get harder and harder, which could put a lot of stress on you. You know your uncle and I want you to do well in school, so you can make something of yourself. That would make your mom and dad proud."

Robert hugged his aunt, "I promise you, if my grades start slipping or you see that the game is putting too much stress on me, you can pull me out of the contest."

She smiled as a tear ran down her face.

"You would do that for me, Sweety?"

"Of course."

"Alright then, go find your uncle so you won't be late for school."

Robert got up and ran out the door, anxious to leave behind the site of his aunt with tears rolling down her cheeks.

That evening after school, Robert could smell his favorite food cooking as he came into the house. "Strange," he thought, "it's expensive to make and his aunt and uncle had been short on money." He shrugged and headed to his room. He woke up his computer.

Dear Mary,

I know the feeling. I have very few friends also. But we have each other to talk to.

I almost got into a fight with Mark the school bully, but right before he could hit me, Mr. James came out of his science room and walked Mark down to the principal's office.

For some odd reason my aunt is making a favorite meal. I didn't think we had the money for it. Well, I have homework to do. Talk to you later.

Hugs and kisses,

Robert

"Robert! Go clean up for dinner, please." his aunt called. She sounded like she was in a good mood. Relieved and happy, Robert ran to the dining room.

"Well champ, we're having your favorite," his uncle smiled.

His aunt smiled as she put the food on the table, but Robert thought her eyes looked different. Glassy instead of sparkly like they usually were when she smiled.

"So what's the big deal? I thought we didn't have the money for a dinner like this."

"Your aunt and I don't. But I thought you might want a little celebration dinner, so I borrowed a little bit from your winnings when I put it in the bank for you today. I hope you don't mind."

"No, of course I don't mind."

The three of them ate dinner. At first, Robert concentrated on his food, savoring each bite. However, by dessert he became uncomfortable by his aunt's silence. He noticed that she only nodded or replied in one or two word sentences. He hoped she wasn't getting sick.

After dinner Robert went to his room. He was doing his homework when he heard a knock at his door. "Robert may I come in?"

It was his uncle.

"Sure, I'm just finishing up my homework."

His uncle walked in and sat beside him. "I got a call today about some person named Mark trying to pick a fight with you."

"I swear I didn't do anything. He was mad because I won the contest."

"I know. I got the whole story from the principal. You did right by not getting into a fight with him. But that was not the real reason I came in to talk to you. I can tell that you saw your aunt is acting differently."

His uncle went quiet for a moment and then continued. "Well when she heard about the fight, it sent her over the edge. She went and saw a special doctor who put her on medicine to calm her nerves."

"I'm really sorry if I made her sick."

"No…no. It's not you. This is just bringing back memories of her brother and she's having a hard time with it."

"Please let her know that will never happen to me."

His uncle laughed, "I already have, champ. Oh, by the way, did you see that box sitting on your bed?"

Robert looked over at his bed and saw a flat box with a computer company's name on it.

Robert looked at his uncle and then at the box again. "Could it be?" Robert thought to himself as he walked over to the box and started to open it.

"Hold on a minute, champ. I want your aunt to see this also."

Robert's uncle gave a yell for Sally. Sally rushed in.

"Well, Robert, open it!" she said in a soft voice.

Robert opened the box and it was better than he imagined. It was a new laptop computer. The newest model. "Wow," was all he could say.

Sally sat on the edge of the bed and patted it to motion Robert sit by her. Robert sat and looked at her expectantly. She, in turn, looked at his uncle.

"We used part of your money to buy the laptop for two reasons. First, you've needed a new computer for awhile. And second, we wanted to make sure that you can still get your school work and e-mail all of your friends and your mom and dad when we go to Io for the next round of the contest."

"Did they tell you where the final is being held?"

His aunt looked away. His uncle answered, "If you win, we'll be going to a different solar system."

"Do you think I have a chance?"

"As good a chance as anyone else." His uncle patted him on the back, then put his arm around his aunt.

Robert kissed his aunt's cheek and hugged his uncle. Then his uncle led his aunt out of the room, leaving Robert with his new computer.

Robert took the computer out of the box and gently opened it. He started it up, amazed at how much faster it was than his old computer. First he wrote to his mother and father, then to Timmy, but he saved the best for last.

Dear Mary,

I know I don't usually write to you more than once a day, but I just had to let you know I got a laptop. So when I go to Io for the next tourney, I will still be able to write you.

Love always

Rob

***

Weeks passed. Robert and Mary still wrote to each other, but Robert's letters were more about the shots and medicine that Robert was taking to get ready for his long space trip. He got a couple letters from his mom and dad, saying how proud they were of him. Mary would send a picture now and then of the new ships that were landing in port.

The day to leave for Io finally arrived. The last thing Robert remembered of earth was the nurse giving him a shot right before he climbed into a sleep chamber. The next thing Robert remembered was waking up and being shown that they were orbiting around Io. Robert was very excited. As before, they were escorted to a luxury hotel and everything was on the house. As before, they ate a tasty dinner and retired so that Robert could rest for the tournament.

Early the next morning, Robert was shuffled off to a very long day of battling his opponents. There were only sixteen contestants left, but the systems had been upgraded and the battles were much more intense. After the tournament, Robert rushed to his room to write Mary a letter before he had to go to the celebration dinner. He wanted the detail to be as fresh in his mind as possible.

Dear Mary

Guess what? I won today! I could not believe it. The first thing I found out was that system had been upgraded, which gave me more things I could do. I felt I had more control over my men. The worst battle was the last one I played. I played against an older woman -- older than my aunt. She looked like she might have been in the service with the way she had her hair cut.

Anyway, like I said, at first she was kicking my butt and I was losing ships left and right. I was down to 12 fighting ships and 1 large cruiser. I started with 36 fighter and 4 cruisers, so that's a huge loss of men. Then it dawned on me that I was fighting them in 2D and so was she. So I took it to next level, used my math skill to calculate the X, Y and Z levels and just ran all over her.

I hope to hear from you soon. I have to go to the celebration dinner for my winning.

Love with a hug and kiss,

Robert

Robert quickly changed his clothes and headed over to his aunt's and uncle's hotel room. As he arrived at the door, his uncle stepped out. Robert could hear his aunt crying in the background, saying something about "poor people".

"Isn't Aunt Sally going with us?" he asked.

"Ummm… No, she's not feeling well," his uncle didn't seem quite at ease. "She said she might join us later."

"Oh, okay." Robert didn't want to pressure his uncle into talking about it. It was a night to enjoy, after all. He was going to the final competition.

Robert and his uncle walked to the main floor of the hotel. As soon as they stepped out of the elevator, they were met by four men who escorted them to a large dining room. There were a lot of people there. Robert recognized some of them as the players and their families, but there were others he didn't recognize. As they stepped in, people cheered and clapped.

"This is all for you, Robert," one of the men said. "For you and everyone you battled."

As Robert and his uncle made their way to a long table, people stopped Robert to shake his hand and congratulate him on his big win. Right before they started to eat, his aunt joined them, but she still seemed sick to Robert. Her eyes were glassy and her smile seemed pasted on.

After dessert, two men in Space Navy suits walked down the aisle, along with the lady he had fought for first place. She was also wearing a Space Navy suit. So he had been right, she was in the Space Navy. Robert felt pride well up inside him. He had beaten a real Space Navy Admiral. He remembered how hard her expression had been when he faced her in battle. But now, she had a softer look and a large smile. "Robert, would you come up here for a moment?" she asked.

Robert looked at his uncle and aunt. They both smiled and nodded. Robert walked up the aisle and stood next to the lady.

"Robert, you battled very well today. For that, you get a medal of honor, your ticket for you and your family to the final round, and your prize winning check… But we have a special surprise for you -- your very own Space Navy Admiral uniforms." She handed him three different suits and hats, all emblazoned with the Space Navy and Admiral rank insignias. "Congratulations."

The audience applauded. Robert just stared at the suits. The insignias looked so real.

The party went on for a long time. People came up to congratulate Robert. Other players wanted to know his tactics. It was late when Robert made it back to his room. Robert kissed and hugged his aunt goodnight. His uncle followed him into his room to admire his new suits.

"We have a big trip coming up tomorrow," his uncle said, smoothing out the dress suit on its hanger.

"We're leaving so soon?" Robert asked.

"Yes, we have a long journey ahead of us."

"I need to check my e-mail, but I'll make it quick." Robert opened the lid to his laptop. "Oh, what did Aunt Sally mean by 'poor people' earlier?"

His uncle looked at him, surprised and then started to laugh.

"You know your aunt! Always tender-hearted. We were talking about how sad it is that the people on a space station can't have pets."

"Ah..," Robert creased his eyebrows together, thinking how lonely he'd be without Hamlet jumping up beside him and knocking things over. "That is sad."

His uncle shook his hand, "Good night, Admiral Robert."

"Good night, Uncle Sam."

Robert checked his e-mail and found that he had three new ones: one from his parents, one from his friend Timmy and one from Mary. Robert opened Mary's first.

Dear Robert,

I saw you on TV today at your party. You looked so cute up there. Oh and guess what? Where you're going for the final round is close to Mobius 9. I talked to my mom and dad. If we can, we will come watch you at the finals and I will be able to give you that hug and kiss!

Love always and forever,

Mary

Robert smiled from ear to ear. He read the other two messages, but they didn't really sink in. He would finally get a hug and kiss from Mary. He went to sleep, dreaming of how soft her lips would be against his own.

His uncle woke him early in the morning to help him get ready to go. He told him to wear his Space Navy dress uniform to the ship. "You'll be on television again," his uncle said. "It's all part of the show."

As they walked to the ship, his aunt walked beside him, silently wringing her hands.

He reached over and squeezed her hand, "Don't be nervous, Aunt Sally. I'm not." It was a lie, sort of, but if it made her feel better, he figured it was a harmless one.

When they approached the sleep chamber, he saw two space marines standing on either side of the door. They saluted him as he passed by them. He returned the salute and grinned, as they walked in.

"Gosh, Aunt Sally. Isn't it cool how they are treating me like a real Admiral?"

"Yes, Sweety, it's nice," she said in a sweet, but distant, voice.

The doctor was waiting for them in the sleep chamber. He gave them each a shot and secured them in their pods.

***

When Robert woke up and climbed out of his sleep pod, the two space marines were waiting for him at attention. He didn't see his aunt or uncle. They walked down a hallway and stopped at a metal door with a gold plaque that read, Space Navy Admiral Robert Crystal. "How cool can this be?" he asked. Neither answered.

One of the space marines opened the door for him and motioned him inside, "Sir, once you enter, you cannot leave until the mission is over. Do you understand?"

"Yes," Robert answered.

"Please enter, Sir," the other space marine said.

Robert smiled and entered the room. The ceiling and three walls were made of what looked like glass. In front of him were a large leather chair and a console table with a glass wall down its center. An older man sat on the other side of the glass wall, in front of his own console. His opponent looked like a college professor. Robert grinned. This was going to be a piece of cake. To his right and left, the walls were made of glass also, as was the ceiling. He could see rows of people watching from behind the glass. His aunt and uncle smiled and waved, but he looked everywhere and couldn't see Mary. A speaker came to life. Robert almost jumped out of his skin.

"Welcome, Space Navy fans. This is the final mission. Admiral Robert Crystal is here today to save our worlds. If he fails, they will be overrun, sending us into slavery. The alien controls will be manned by his opponent, Steven Bernard."

Robert thought, "This is too cool! It seems so real." He checked over his controls carefully, wanting to make sure he didn't make a fool of himself. Since it was the last round, he was sure they were televising it on live TV.

The announcer turned his attention to the contestants. "You have full control of your ships. However, once you have made a choice, there is no turning back. The people under your command will follow your every order. You will also notice that you have some new controls. Use them if needed."

Robert nodded and sat down at his console, looking over the new controls: Statistical Predictions and Planet Buster Beam. He looked over to the other player's console. From what he could tell, he had about the same layout. He watched his opponent studying the controls. Robert smiled when he saw that the man had an old fashion hearing aid like his grandfather wore. He thought it funny that a person old enough to be his grandfather would still be playing video games.

Then the 3D map came to life. He could see a lot of dull red enemy dots, a few blue Space Navy dots, and a world shown as blue. He called up a read-out of his mission, the resources he had available, and what he was up against.

"This is Planet 131529211909. It has been overrun by 200,000 aliens. The enemy has deployed every ship they have to confront us. Your resources are limited to 13 war galleys and 300 fighters. We cannot afford to leave the other planets wide open, to save a single colony. You must stop the aliens with the resources provided. Good luck."

The speaker clicked off.

Robert took a closer look at the war galleys. They all had names, which was something new. One caught his eye -- the USS Hatter. He smiled and thought, "Wow they're even using real ships names. That's the one mom and dad are on."

He pushed the button to contact the ship, "Report Captain of the USS Hatter. How many enemy ships are out there?"

A cracking sound came over the speaker, "We are outnumbered at least 10 to 1, Sir. Maybe more."

Robert started to sweat a bit. This was going to be hard one.

"Is it correct that Planet 131529211909 has over 200,000 alien on it?"

"That is correct, Sir."

"How many of our people?"

"25,000 civilians, Sir."

Robert weighed the matter and then smiled. He'd never been able to actually talk to the ships' captains before. "Captain, you will only take orders from me. I will use you to lead the battle."

"Yes, Sir, Admiral Crystal."

Robert's mind was spinning. He had always imagined that he and his parents would work together on a space galley. This was all too cool.

"How far away are the enemy ships from the planet?" Robert asked.

"They will come out of warp all around the planet in one minute."

Robert activated the planet buster button on his console.

"Are you and the other galleys in position to use the planet buster if necessary?"

"Yes, Sir!" The man sounded a little nervous.

Robert laughed to himself, "Of course this can't be my father. My father would never sound nervous."

"Don't worry, Captain. I know what I am doing."

"Yes sir! That is why you're the admiral."

"Switch all control of the planet buster beams over to me."

"Sir?"

"Do as I say. I don't mind getting my hands dirty."

"Yes, Sir."

"Did we get a chance to get any of our people off the planet?"

"No, sir."

He pressed the Statistical Prediction button, "Computer, the damage and loss to the enemy if the planet was destroyed as they left warp."

"Enemy loss would be 60% if one shot was fired. The colony would be destroyed." Robert figured what losses there would be on the planet; how all 25,000 would die and their pets . He reminded himself that it is only a game. There are no real people and no real pets on the planet.

"Would I lose the game?"

"No, the loss of civilian lives is not counted in the score. The score is calculated based on loss of your military resources versus loss of the alien's military resources."

Robert sat back in his chair and felt a little more at ease. "Computer, what would be my losses if I had my ships channel most of their power to the front deflector shields?"

"There would be a chance of a 2% loss."

Robert smiled, knowing that what he was about to do was going to throw the old guy for a loop.

He pressed the communication button for the USS Hatter, "On my command, instruct all ships to put all power to their front shields and ride out the wave."

"Yes Sir!"

Robert saw the old man jump from his chair, his face red. His hearing aid popped out of his ear and Robert saw that it was not a hearing aid, but was attached to the console. By the old man's expression, Robert figured he had heard the commands Robert had given. Robert could not believe this, they had made the mission extremely hard and now they were cheating.

"Cheater!" he screamed at the man, forgetting his communication channel was still open.

"Sir?"

"Nothing, Captain. We will continue as planned,"

Robert's eyes narrowed, watching the red dots grow larger. The older man ran to the window and beat on it, shaking his head no.

"Ten seconds, Sir."

159

Robert lifted his finger from his communication button and eyed the old man, "What's the matter, cheater? You didn't think I had the balls to kill my own people. And that's the only way to win. This contest was rigged, but it's only a game. Relax and feel your loss."

He pressed the communication button, "Shields up. Once the blast wave has passed, have your fighters attack the alien ships that are left."

The red dots turned a bright red. The enemy ships were out of warp. Robert pressed three of the planet buster buttons -- overkill, from the computer's statistics, but it should do what he hoped.

Robert heard static from the speakers, but in the background he thought he heard someone say, "My god, he killed all of those civilians."

He watched the blue planet disappear along with most of the enemy ships. The old man turned, shaking his head, and fell into his chair. He placed his face in his hands. Robert smiled. He had won and made a grown man cry. He could only faintly hear the yells of applause behind the glass walls and ceiling.

Robert pressed the Report button, "Computer, what is the loss to the enemy? And to my ships?"

"Well done, Admiral. 90 percent of the enemy ships were destroyed. None of yours were reported lost, sir."

Robert could not help but laugh. He pressed the button for the USS Hatter, "Captain, send your fighters to destroy the remaining ships. Lead the galleys to all enemy outposts and then their home world. Destroy them all."

"But sir, we have defeated them."

"Do as I command. That will be my final order."

160

There is a pause, then the voice acknowledged the command, "Yes sir."

"Computer, cut off all communication with these Space Navy ships. They may only speak to each other until they have fulfilled their mission. Also, translate the name of the planet. I would like to take it off my star map at home. "

The com light went off and Robert smiled at himself. He was sure Mr. Bernard hadn't expected that. He watched as the numbers started turning into letters.

```
13 --- M
15 --- O
2 ---- B
```

Robert's eyes started to widen.

```
9 ---- I
```

Robert was getting a real bad feeling about this.

```
21 --- U
19 --- S
```

Terror started rising up in Robert's blood.

```
09 ---09
```

Robert felt his hands shake and sweat ran down his forehead. He tried to control the panic that welled up around his heart, "This is just a game and only a game," he thought to himself.

"Computer, unlock my door and have the game controller come in." His voice cracked.

In a few moments he heard his door slide open and the man who had given his uncle the tickets and money at the house stepped in with a big smile. He wore a Space Navy dress suit like Robert's.

He extended his hand, "Well done, Admiral. You saved the human race. I must admit, your technique was unusual, but effective."

Robert let out an unsure laugh. "I won the game, right?"

"You might say that."

"It was just a very vivid game, right?" Robert's voice broke in deep and high-pitched tones.

"War is just a game adults play," the man motioned for the space marines to step into the room.

Robert looked through the glass at his aunt and uncle and the other onlookers. His aunt was passed out; his uncle was weeping. He looked at the old man on the other side of the glass, still crying in his console chair. He remembered what his aunt had said at Io space station and, slowly, he realized what was happening.

Hoping he was wrong, he addressed the console, "Computer, pull up the listing of the people who were on the planet."

A large list appeared on the 3D screen. But one name screamed out at him – the one name he'd hoped he wouldn't see.

Mary Ann Carver --DEAD AT THE AGE OF 14

Robert felt something heavy around his shoulder. An arm identical to his in color and insignia rested across his back, "Admiral Crystal, those people died so many others could live. Sometimes there must be sacrifices."

Robert dropped to his knees, his mind unable to reconcile what he had done. He had killed the one he loved and committed genocide. He felt hands wrap around his arms and, slowly, his world went black.

***

"Captain, you and your son did an excellent job."

"Thank you, sir. May I see him now?"

"Of course, of course."

A man in a Space Navy suit followed an older man in a white doctor's coat.

"You understand you can only see him through the window."

"Yes, I know."

"Is your wife having a hard time with this? I notice she didn't come."

"Oh no, she's just getting the troops ready for our next mission."

The doctor nodded. They walked up to a window. The room was painted bright white and everything was very clean. Through the window, they could hear the soft music playing in the room. Robert's father saw that Robert struggled against the straps that held him to the bed. A stain on his cheek showed the trail of tears that had been running since they'd admitted him.

"I wonder what he is thinking."

"We don't know. We do know that he has a very strong mind. Something inside his mind is keeping it active, so the mind wipes are going to take time."

"Mind wipes?"

"Yes, with the hope we can reprogram him to being close to himself again."

"Well, yes. Mind wipes are standard protocol now, aren't they?" the father looked at his young son and felt pride. "Better than the scars that plagued the soldiers of the past."

The doctor nodded. The Captain turned and walked away.

The doctor stood and listened to the boy's rambling, "I must count every last one of them I murdered, 596 people on a galley ship, 2 people on each fighter, 39 known worlds of alien people and their pets. Yes I believe they would have had pets...…1…..Mary…………2.…..I'm so sorry ….3….Mary….."

A tear ran down Roberts face, following the well-worn trail.

The Leaf Man

By Rachelle Reese

Rebecca

Rebecca woke up dripping with sweat, the night still calm and dark around her. Jerry lay snoring, grasping the edge of his side of the bed. More nights than not had been like this lately. "Perimenopause," Rebecca convinced herself again. She was in her mid forties, after all. And as for Jerry…maybe he was going through the change of life too. Some say men do. Rebecca turned onto her back and reached out toward her husband. He grunted a little and rolled over toward her, placing his hand over her left breast. Rebecca drifted back to sleep, not exactly where she had been, but close enough. Too close.

She heard the noise around the same time the dogs did. Something heavy clanking down the gravel road. Something being dragged. Something large. It's started, *the wind spoke clearly.* What's started? *she asked.* The nightmare. *The clouds circled around the words laughing.* My nightmare? *She asked the wind. Her only answer was a scream.*

Rebecca opened her eyes to daylight streaming in through the windows. Jerry was already up. There had been times many years ago that she would have sought him out to tell him about her dream, but they didn't communicate on that level anymore. They didn't communicate much at all since the Carters had sold their land to the developer. She put her arm around Tuxedo, the black and white mutt who'd shown up in their driveway a few years before. He rolled over and licked her face. "Not now, Tuxedo," she said. "I overslept." Rebecca climbed out of bed and put on sweat pants and an oversized shirt decorated with paint splotches. She had a show in a month and nothing new done. She walked past her studio, carefully avoiding the four unfinished canvases mounted on easels. "Coffee first, then paint."

Rebecca poured herself a cup of coffee and stepped out onto the front porch. Halloween and Taboo greeted her with their black backs arched. Pandora, the grey tabby cat, jumped up on the railing, anxious for food. "Are you telling me you're hungry?" Rebecca asked, scratching each cat on the back of the neck. "Be right back." She went inside and got some dry cat food, pouring small piles along the railing and a larger pile on the ground. More cats would be in later and most of them preferred to eat alone.

Cats fed and coffee in hand, Rebecca could find no more excuses. She stepped inside her studio and sat down at a canvas. A man glared back at her, his face sculpted inside the bark of the tree. "I thought I got rid of you yesterday," Rebecca murmured. "Why are you back again?" She picked up a brush and dipped it in light brown paint, eager to spread it over the man-face she'd never intended to paint. The man she'd never known except in dreams – until now. And now he was in all the canvases. In the bark of a tree, the rivulets on a lake, the shadows between the stalks of summer corn, and even in the wings of the butterfly hovering around the Rose of Sharon one last time before the frost. Rebecca looked at the canvas again – and still the little man's face stared back, grinning now not glaring. "Well, at least he's happy now," she thought, taking a sip of her coffee. Maybe today wouldn't be such a good day to paint. Besides, they were low on groceries and it was turning cold. She really should track down some firewood and warm clothes. The paintings would be there tomorrow.

Rebecca showered and changed into town clothes. She told the dogs to be good and left, shutting the door to her studio behind her. She drove with the windows down, even though it was cool. She loved the feel of autumn on her cheeks – freedom. Curve by curve she drove down the gravel road. Huge beasts roamed over what used to be the Carters' property. Huge metal beasts, scooping up dirt, knocking down trees, changing what once would have been trees flaming in autumn reds and yellows into brown and sullen dirt. And suddenly before her, the man from her paintings sat squarely in the middle of the road, legs and arms crossed as if to block her path, clean-shaven wrinkled face scowling. Rebecca screamed and swerved to miss him, slamming the car into the trunk of a tree. Then black…then black.

"Wake up, Rebecca," the man leaned over her. "It's not over yet. And you can help us."

Rebecca opened her eyes. A large bearded man hovered over her, "Y'uns okay ma'am? You need us to call an ambulance?"

"No." Rebecca struggled to get out of the car. The last thing she needed today was to end up in a hospital with a bunch of incompetent doctors. "I'm fine."

The man offered her a hand and she took it, feeling the swoon as he pulled her to her feet.

"You sure you're okay ma'am?"

"I'm fine," she insisted. "How's the car?"

"Totaled, I'd say," the man shook his head. "Why'd you swerve off the road, anyway?"

"There was a man…" Rebecca started to say.

"A man?"

"A man in the road," But even as she said it, she knew there had been no man in the road.

"You're mistaken, ma'am. There weren't no man in the road."

"Yes. I must have been mistaken," Rebecca looked at the demolished hillside and saw the man standing on the top of the hill. "Do you think one of you could drive me home? I only live a few miles down the road."

"Sorry ma'am, we're on the clock. Be happy to let you use my cell phone, though."

"That's okay. I'll walk." Rebecca started off down the road.

"Hey ma'am, what about the car?"

"I'll call a tow truck for it after I get home." Rebecca started off toward her house, glancing behind her one last time. The man was no longer on the top of the hill. Who knows, maybe she had dreamed him. She hadn't been sleeping well, after all. Damn night sweats. She dreaded telling Jerry about the car. He had been so wrapped up about money lately. Replacing her car would be the last straw. Well, technically he wouldn't *need* to replace it. She didn't really use the car that much anyway. Not since the incident – of course, she'd never told Jerry about the incident.

Rebecca shivered and pushed the memory out of her mind. There were just some things it was better not to face. She walked. Up hill and down hill. With each step, it seemed her body became heavier. And her head hurt more. At least the man was nowhere around. Her illusory stalker. And at least it wasn't cold. Rebecca sank down into a pile of fallen leaves just off the road. A short rest and then she'd walk again.

Don't let him do it. She felt a wet warmth cover her ear and jerked awake. "Oh god, Hooch! What are you doing this far from home?" She reached over to give her whiskey-colored mutt a hug. "What am I saying? You haven't been home for days, have you? You have a woman friend around here, huh?" She ruffled the back of his neck.

Hooch whined, then ran to a spot in the leaves and started digging. A few minutes later, he lifted his treasure from the leaves. Rebecca screamed. Hooch held what looked like a human skull in his teeth. "Give me that!"

Hooch growled and ran away, still clutching his treasure.

Rebecca struggled to her feet to follow. Dizziness threatened, but she pressed on, stumbling through the tree branches blown over by the summer storms, slipping on new-fallen leaves. Hooch led her to the back edge of their land. The edge against the road she never traveled. Hooch dropped the skull at the trunk of a tree and then she saw it. The For Sale sign nailed to the tree. "Bastard," she thought, anger building inside of her. "Money hungry bastard." She grasped the sign and ripped it out of the tree, surprised at her own strength. "Are there more, boy? Show me." She picked up the sign and carried it along with her. She would confront Jerry about this tonight, headache or not.

Hooch took her to three more signs and she tore each one off the tree. When the last one came down, she sank into a pile of leaves beneath the tree and drifted into an exhausted, pain-laced sleep. Hooch stretched out beside her and put his head on her thigh. When she woke, the day had given way to evening. A half moon hung bright in the southern sky. *Moon of justice.* The wind sang in her ears. *Moon of balance.* Rebecca gathered the signs and started her long walk through the woods, Hooch beside her, wishing she too had fur to keep her warm.

****

When Rebecca reached the top of the hill overlooking their house, she could tell that Jerry was home because the television cast its strange shadows across their bedroom window. She wondered if he had noticed the crashed car on his way home. A part of her hoped he had and that he was worried about her. Another part knew he had and that he wasn't. She rehearsed the words she would say when she laid the signs down on the coffee table in front of him. Then she headed swiftly down the hill, anxious to be warm again.

Hooch bounded past the row of cats, up the stairs, and to the front door. Rebecca followed as quickly as she could, but tired and burdened with the signs, she was too slow for Hooch. He started to bark. By the time Rebecca made it up the steps, she could see the Jerry's silhouette moving down the hallway toward the door. She could tell he was on the phone. He swung open the door just as she reached the bottom of the steps. Hooch ran inside, heading straight for the food bowl no doubt. The door closed as she reached the top of the steps. "A warm welcome, just what I expected," she thought. "I guess he saw the car." She felt anger and tears well up in her throat. She swung open the door and stepped inside, slamming the door behind her. As its echo died away, she heard the phone hit the floor and suddenly Jerry's arms were around her. The signs fell to the floor near her feet.

"Oh my God. You're home. Rebecca….I saw the car and I thought….I've been calling hospitals and I couldn't bring myself to call the morgue. But you're safe." He squeezed her so tight that the pain she hadn't felt all day overwhelmed her.

"Careful," she gasped, half collapsing inside his arms. "I hurt."

He loosened his grip and drew her toward the kitchen. "Let me look at you."

"I'm okay," she said. "Just sore."

"Let me see," he ran his fingers across her face. "Your face is pretty bruised. Where else do you hurt?"

"Everywhere," she admitted, her anger diffused by his touch. "Are you mad about the car?"

"I could give a fuck about the car. I was worried about you. My Becca."

Rebecca felt tears in her eyes, "You haven't called me that in years."

"You'll always be My Becca. No one else's." He pulled her close again, this time more gently. "Oh God. I'm just glad you're safe." Rebecca felt moisture on her shoulders and realized her husband was crying.

Jerry was tender with her that night like he hadn't been in years. First he bathed her, gently washing away the grime, inspecting every bruise. After he'd bundled her into her warm fuzzy robe and slippers, he poured her a drink and made her dinner. He even lit the candles on the table. Rebecca was careful not to bring up the signs. That discussion would wait until morning. She was too sore, too tired, and enjoying the pampering too much to ruin the mood.

When they went to bed, they snuggled close. He ran his fingers gently over her face, as if feeling it for the first time. "That's the only way my father ever saw my mother," he said. "He felt her face and knew she was beautiful."

"You still miss him, don't you?" Rebecca asked.

"I'll always miss him."

"I know," Rebecca sighed. "I wish I could have known him."

"I love you," Jerry put his mouth on hers and they shared a long and tender kiss. "Do you feel up to making love?"

"I think so. But be gentle." She ran her hand down his back and marveled that his muscles were still so firm. Most of their friends had become plump with age, but not Jerry. She supposed it was his Indian heritage. His father had been slender and fit right up until the end.

"You are so beautiful," he whispered and ran his fingertips down her neck, around her breasts, over her belly, and finally between her thighs. She felt the thrill run through her like it used to long ago. She pulled his pelvis toward hers and when they both were ready, they made love, rocking together slowly at first, shutting out the world, drifting over the gentle waves, far out to sea. Then the tide rose and they were flung together high on the surf, riding it in to shore. Exuberant in their mutual conquest, they rose up higher, higher until finally the wave broke over them and left them clinging together, exhausted from its thrust.

They lay together, arms and legs entwined, neither one ready to let go of the other, having found each other again after so long. Tuxedo whined, pacing along the edge of the bed. "Relax, Tuxedo," Rebecca said. "We still love you." She patted the empty area of the bed beside her and felt Tuxedo land lightly. He circled around a few times, and then settled on a position with his back toward her. Rebecca laid her head on Jerry's chest. He was already starting to snore lightly. She closed her eyes and let his even breathing lull her to sleep.

****

Her hands sifted through the leathery brown oak leaves. They were too old to be pretty, but not old enough to crumble at her touch. She was looking for something, but couldn't remember what she'd lost. She'd remember when she found it, she told herself. Then she felt it. Something circular and metal. Her ring. She pulled it up out of the leaves and placed it on her ring finger. As she did, she felt the solid rock beneath her dissolve and she was falling, falling, falling. And all around her, it was raining leaves. Leathery brown, brilliant red, and bright fluttering yellow. They drifted slowly alongside her. One grinned and winked. Another giggled. A small red one screamed as if terrified by the fall. And another screamed, and another and the giggles turned to screams as they plummeted, one face and then another, no longer suspended by the wind. And she fell too. "It's not over," the man's voice called out. "Tell him it won't end his way." Rebecca grasped for something, anything to keep from falling. She closed her eyes and let out a scream. And then she landed. Sharp sticks pricked at her naked flesh. She started to throw them aside, searching for the softness of autumn leaves, spring grass, anything other than these sticks. She opened her eyes and picked up a stick to throw it. It was white, not brown. And a hollow ran down its center. A hollow that had once been life. She held a bone – a child-sized tibia. Rebecca screamed, throwing it aside and looked around. She was lying in a field of bones. Skulls, arms, ribs, legs, fingers. Some were human. Others were not. She picked up a skull that looked like it might have belonged to a large dog. "Coyote," the skull spoke. "I was a coyote. I have no food to hunt, no water to drink. And so my spirit waits."

"You can speak?"

"You're dreaming," the skull answered. "Dreams have no language barriers."

"Why do you wait?"

"I wait for you. You will be the one who decides."

"Decides what?"

"Whether they live or die."

"Who?"

"Our children, our grandchildren, our get."

"Why me?"

"If not you, who? They are starving. They cannot wait forever."

She felt small tongues lapping at her feet.

174

"They are hungry, Rebecca."

She hurled the skull as far as she could throw it and nothing could silence her scream.

"Becca?" Rebecca felt herself being shaken gently. "Are you hurting, honey? Do you need something?"

Rebecca opened her eyes. "Jerry." She looked down toward her feet and saw Tuxedo licking gently between her toes.

"You were screaming. I thought maybe you needed aspirin or something."

"Water," she lifted her head. "Yes, some aspirin. I think the stress from the crash is settling into my muscles."

"Be right back." Jerry climbed out of bed and came back a few minutes later with aspirin and a glass of water.

"You'll think I'm crazy," Rebecca said, "but I had this dream about falling and leaves turning to faces. And then I landed in a field of bones. And this coyote skull talked to me and told me that I would decide who lived or died. And then there were these tongues…well, that was probably just Tuxedo."

"You had a pretty traumatic day today. It's probably because of the accident. Just come here, cuddle up, and get some sleep."

"Okay," Rebecca laid her head on Jerry's chest. She listened as his breathing slowed and the soft snoring began. She tried to synchronize her breathing with his, hoping the slow and steady pace would help her go back to sleep. Finally, she gave up and got out of bed. She put on a painting shirt and sweats and went to her studio. Maybe if she worked for awhile, she'd relax enough to sleep. She propped a new canvas onto yet another easel. If she didn't

175

finish something soon, she'd need to buy more easels, she grimaced. She would work in oil tonight. She chose her colors and squirted them onto a palette. She dipped her brush first in rust, then in brown, and then touched her brush to the canvas. The world eroded away and she became her brush. Swiping, dabbing, swiping. On and on she painted, not noticing that Tuxedo and Hooch had come into the studio and stood behind her watching. And finally, the rising sun cast her new painting in its red glow and she realized it was finished.

A coyote stared back at her from the canvas, thin and restless. It wore a coat of autumn leaves, but around the ribs, the leaves had fallen to the ground leaving the bones of the rib cage exposed. As she studied the painting, she heard two howls behind her and jumped. She turned her head slowly. Tuxedo and Hooch both sat erect, noses pointed to the ceiling, letting out the most awful howls she'd ever heard.

"Fine, you two don't like it," Rebecca scolded. "Well at least it's finished. One down….well, never mind. Let's go see if your father's made coffee." Rebecca started to leave the room, then noticed the two of them weren't leaving. She went over and patted Hooch on the head. He snapped at her and for a second she saw murder in his eyes. Then his eyes returned to normal and he licked her hand. She was more cautious with Tuxedo. He was a nervous dog under the best of circumstances. "Tuxedo," she called. "Come here boy. He didn't change his pose or stop his howl. "Tuxedo, food." Still no change. Hooch walked up to Tuxedo and sniffed around his muzzle, then let out a shrill bark. Tuxedo stopped howling and looked confused for a moment. He cocked his head to one side, then looked from Rebecca, to the painting, then back to Rebecca. Finally, he chose Rebecca and ran toward her, bounding between her outstretched arms and nearly knocking her over. Rebecca petted him and pushed him back gently, "It's okay, boy. You come with me. That painting will be dried and boxed up in two days. Then you never have to look at it again. Let's go get a treat."

Rebecca started toward the kitchen with both dogs trailing close behind her. She was surprised to find that coffee had not been made. In fact, there was no sign that Jerry was awake at all. She looked at the clock, 7:00. He was usually up by now. She gave the dogs each a rawhide bone and started coffee. Then she went back to the bedroom. Jerry was still sleeping soundly. She leaned over and kissed his forehead. He jumped, then opened his eyes, "What was that for?"

"Time to wake up, sleepy head."

"I mean the kiss. You haven't kissed my forehead in the morning in years."

"You just looked so peaceful lying there asleep, I couldn't resist."

"What time is it?"

"Seven. I started coffee."

"What are you doing awake?"

"I couldn't sleep, so I painted. I finished it."

"Which one?"

"A new one. The dogs don't like it though."

"What's it called?"

She looked puzzled for a moment and then it came to her, "Hunger."

"Odd name for a painting."

177

"Well, if you get out of bed, you can see it and then you'll understand."

"I'd rather do other things," he reached his hand out and stroked her breast.

"Me too, but you have to go to work."

"Tonight?" his eyes pleaded.

"Let's see how I feel," Rebecca rubbed her neck. She could feel the stiffness creeping in through her neck and between her shoulder blades and she secretly wished she could just crawl into bed. But that would have to wait. Today she had to deal with getting the car towed, insurance claims, and all the other hassle that comes with wrecking a car.

"Alright," Jerry sighed and climbed out of bed. "Let's see this painting you did." He put on his robe and started toward her studio. She hurried after him. Even when they were arguing, Jerry was a good critic. She was anxious to hear his opinion on this one.

When she walked into the room, she saw him staring intently at one of the other paintings. "That's not the one. It's not finished yet."

"I can see that. But I know that man."

"What man?" she asked, although she already knew the answer.

"The man in the bark."

"Who is it?" she asked.

"An old friend of my father's. But you couldn't have known him. Weird."

"What was his name?"

"I don't remember. I only met him a few times. And I was very young."

"What was he like?"

"Crazy as they come. He was a medicine man or something when he was younger, but by the time I knew him, they'd put him away in a mental hospital. Paranoid delusional or something."

Rebecca felt a chill. "Is he still alive?"

"Beats me. I can't imagine he would be though. He wasn't a young man when I knew him."

"Strange coincidence, I guess. Besides, it's not finished. I'll probably end up painting him out." Rebecca put her hand on Jerry's elbow and guided him to her new painting. "Come look at the finished one."

Jerry looked at the painting without saying a word.

"Well, what do you think?"

Finally, he moved toward it and ran his finger around the coyote's eyes, not touching the canvas, yet feeling it as a three-dimensional shape. "You've captured him exactly. His bone structure is just as it was in life. What photo did you use?"

"Photo? I just painted. It's not based on a photo."

"Becca, I don't know how you did it, but you painted my father. It's like he's standing right in front of me."

"Jerry, I painted a coyote."

"No, Becca. The leaves are a ruse. He looks like a coyote, but he's really a man. Look at the bone structure. He's really my father. Right down to the cloudy, blind eyes. He seems to be looking at you, but he really sees nothing. It's beautiful." He leaned over and kissed her lightly. "Thank you."

Rebecca looked at the painting, trying to see what Jerry saw. She saw only the coyote, leaves falling from its ribs, leaving it skeletal, starving, only bones.

Jerry

Jerry arrived at the office a little later than usual, but still before the rest of his staff. He'd always liked to be the first one there. Get some coffee. Get settled in. Get focused before the endless stream of people and their problems came streaming through his door. There were definitely some days Jerry wondered why he'd ever become a psychiatrist. Of course, most of it was easy now with the new drugs on the market. Find a combination the patient could tolerate. That was the key. And in the meantime, hope that nothing went seriously wrong.

Jerry looked at the plain brown envelope that sat squarely in the center of his desk. He knew what it was – an offer for the back half of the land. An offer he'd be stupid to refuse. He'd received it not long before the police had called about the car and he hadn't thought much about it. When he got the call, he'd been angry at first, then frantic as he called person after person looking for Rebecca. By the time she stormed through the door, For Sale signs falling from her hands, he'd almost given up. He'd called her friends, her family, the hospital. The only number he hadn't called was the morgue. He was so relieved when he saw her that he hadn't even noticed the For Sale signs until Hooch had growled at them. And by then he didn't care. His wife, his Becca, was alive.

The plain brown envelope stared back at him accusingly. "You need her signature, that's all," he tried to convince himself. The two of them would be able to retire early, travel, do what they'd always talked about doing when they were younger. It was a lot of money. She'd understand.

"Will she?" a voice asked from across his desk. The voice was one he'd never forget.

"Dad?"

"Look at me the way I see things. The way I showed you to see."

Jerry reached across his desk and felt around. Gradually, he felt the features take shape as they had this morning when he'd looked at Rebecca's painting. "Dad! I've missed you so much."

"If you'd missed me enough, we wouldn't be having this conversation," he felt a strong, small hand grasp his and pull it down into arm wrestling position.

"What do you mean?"

The envelope shot across the desk and landed on the floor.

"Dad, you don't understand. It's a lot of money."

"It's a lot of trash. That land is sacred and you know it." Jerry felt his arm giving way and pushed back.

"The land *was* sacred, Dad. The Indians are long gone. Even your friend Running with…"

"Running with Dogs is still running with dogs. And he is *not* crazy."

"Dad…things have changed," Jerry pled, glancing furtively at the plain brown envelope.

"No, son. Things have not changed, only people have." Jerry's outstretched hand fell empty, hitting against the desk. No pressure held it down.

181

Jerry reached for one of the sample Xanax packets in his upper left drawer. "Stress," he told himself. "Just stress." After all, he'd thought Becca was dead for a good part of the evening. And then her painting this morning unnerved him. A coyote of all things. Had he ever told her his father's Indian name was Blind Coyote? He didn't think so, but possibly. He had talked a lot about his father when he first died.

Jerry remembered that day clearly. He and Becca had been dating only a few months, but they knew they were in love. One night Becca asked him what his parents were like. Jerry had looked at her strangely and said, "I can't even remember my father's face." The next day he got the phone call. His father had been cutting down trees on the land and one had fallen on him, smashing his face. Jerry had gotten on the plane and flown home, but his father hadn't regained consciousness. They kept him on life support until the family could all get there. Jerry had watched the bleeps on the monitors and understood what they meant. But still, he'd sat there talking to his father, reading to him as if he could say something that would bring him back. One night, Jerry drifted to sleep holding his father's hand. "Take me off this goddamn thing," his father's voice rang loud and clear. "Just let me rest." The next morning, Jerry talked to the doctors and they confirmed what he already knew. Jerry gathered his mother and his two sisters and explained to them that Dad would never wake up. He encouraged them to let Dad go. It took a few days, each one sitting for hours, holding the dying man's hand, watching the bleeps on the monitor. But on the fifth day, they turned off the machinery and let him pass. To this day, Jerry remembers hearing coyotes call from hill to hill as the spirit of the man he loved passed on.

Jerry picked up the brown envelope off the floor and put it in his desk drawer. He'd bide his time, he decided. There was too much going on right now. He checked his calendar and was relieved to see he didn't have an appointment until 10. That would give him time to call the insurance company. He'd told Rebecca he'd handle it. She was sore and tired. It was better that she spend the day in bed. Jerry picked up the phone and dialed. After a few rings the agent's secretary answered, "Tom Kranston Insurance".

"Anita? It's Jerry. Is Tom around?"

"Sure, Jerry. Hold on." A few seconds later Tom picked up the phone.

"What can I do for you Jerry? Buy a new car?"

"No, Tom. Unfortunately Rebecca had a little accident."

"Is she alright?"

"Fortunately yes. At least I think so. She's pretty bruised and sore, but she didn't want to go to the hospital. However, the car is probably totaled. It's at the dealership for an estimate. I'll let you know."

"What happened? Any other vehicles involved?"

"No. No other vehicles. It happened out on County Road 540. You know, where the Carters used to live? She swerved to miss something in the road, lost control and hit a tree."

"What'd she swerve to miss?"

"Well, if you ask her, she'll tell you it was a man sitting Indian style in the road. But it was nothing really. Probably a branch or a pile of leaves. They've been bulldozing a lot of trees for the new construction. You know Rebecca's imagination. You see a tree, she sees an old friend she hasn't seen in years."

"Yeah," Tom chuckled. "Those creative types. I guess that's what makes her an artist. As long as no one was hurt."

"No. There was a construction worker who witnessed it. He confirmed that there was no one else involved."

"Think we can get that in writing?" Tom asked.

"The police already have it. I'll have them forward a copy to you."

"Thanks, Jerry. You just send me that estimate when you get it. And remind Rebecca that if she has any aches and pains that last more than a couple days, she really should see a doctor and get them documented."

"I'll do that." Jerry laughed. "Not that she'll listen."

Both men laughed and said their goodbyes.

Jerry looked at his watch. Half an hour until his first appointment. He'd have time to review the client's file and have another cup of coffee. He opened his desk and pulled the thick file. Clyde Barrett. Paranoid Schizophrenic. Diagnosed five years ago after he attacked his wife with a cattle prod. He claimed God had come to him disguised as an oak tree and told him his wife should suffer for selling some land to a developer. Barrett. Sure. His wife is Rhonda Barrett, one of the best real estate agents in town. In fact, it was her name on the paperwork inside the plain brown envelope on his desk. Jerry continued looking through the file. Successfully medicated from the looks of things. Good. Hopefully it would be just a prescription refill visit.

At 10 am exactly, his intercom rang. "Yes."

"Your 10 o'clock appointment is here."

"Show him in."

As Clyde Barrett stepped into the room, Jerry realized that this would not be a prescription refill visit. Clyde Barrett, normally a clean-shaven man, looked like he hadn't shaved, bathed, or slept in a week or more. His hair was long, unkempt, and littered with dry autumn leaves.

"Have a seat," Jerry motioned to the empty couch. "Or if you'd be more comfortable, take the chair."

"I'm not here to discuss my problems," the man's voice was gravelly. "I'm here to discuss your problems."

Jerry looked furtively at his patient's hands. No weapon that he could see. That was good. "Well, have a seat anyway, Clyde," Jerry said calmly. "We'll just talk man-to-man. About anything you want to talk about."

Clyde Barrett lunged toward the desk and Jerry ducked down behind it instinctively. "I'm here to discuss this."

Jerry looked up over the edge of the desk and saw Clyde Barrett waving the plain brown envelope. He eased back into his seat. "Okay. We can discuss that if you want."

Clyde Barrett ripped the envelope in half and then in half again. Methodically, he tore the envelope and its contents into tiny squares. "No discussion, traitor. Just don't sign." He threw the squares of paper on the floor and left.

Once he was sure Clyde Barrett was out of earshot, Jerry reached for his phone and dialed the police. "Bismarck Police Department, Carl here."

"It's Jerry Evans."

"Jerry, did you find Rebecca?"

"Yes. She made it home last night. Pretty bruised up, but she's fine."

"Good to hear."

"But I'm calling because I need you to check on Rhonda Barrett. Her husband just left my office and I'm afraid he might be off his medication. Given his history…."

"We'll send someone to the real estate office just to make sure."

"Thanks, Carl."

"No problem, Jerry. We appreciate the tip."

Jerry hung up the phone and looked at his empty coffee cup. He debated filling it again, but decided that the way the day had started out, he'd better not get too jittery. He looked at the mess on the floor and called his secretary. "Janet, could you send building maintenance up here?"

"What do you need, Mr. Evans?"

Jerry stood up to survey the mess, "A vacuum cleaner at least." Then he noticed the pattern in the pieces of paper. "On second thought, don't call maintenance yet. Can you run out and buy one of those disposable cameras for me?"

"No need, Mr. Evans. I have a camera on my cell phone."

"Well, bring it here. I want documentation of this." The paper squares had landed in such a way that they spelled:

LEAFMAN

Janet came in with her cell phone. She looked at the mess on the floor. "Not a good day for Mr. Barrett?"

Jerry held out his hand for the camera and beckoned for her to stand beside him. "Look what it says."

"Who's Leafman?"

"Damned if I know."

186

"He sat on the floor and spelled out Leafman in little pieces of paper?"

"No. They just landed like that when he threw them."

"You're joking, right?" Janet took a few shots and showed them to Jerry.

Jerry looked at the snapshots and shook his head, "I wish I was."

Rebecca

After Jerry left, Rebecca had curled up on the couch with Tuxedo and Hooch and tried to rest. But her neck and back ached no matter how she lay. Finally, she gave up and decided to take a long hot bath. She ran water as hot as she could stand it into their Jacuzzi tub. Next she added bath salts, an ice cube of frozen rose petals, and some fresh mint leaves picked from the plant in the kitchen window. She'd read that mint leaves were good for sore muscles. She climbed gingerly over the edge of the tub and sank down slowly into the scented warm water. Almost immediately, she felt the pain flow out of her lower back. She turned on the jets and leaned back. Little by little she felt relief flood through her body. "I could spend all day in here," she thought. She watched the mint leaves and rose petals swirl around her, a hypnotic kaleidoscope of pinks, reds, yellows, and greens. First they were flowers, weaving in and out. Then butterflies fluttering through the leaves, resting briefly on a blossom to suck its nectar. She watched, amused, but careful not to drift off to sleep. She'd always been afraid of drowning in the bathtub.

At last, waterlogged and relaxed, Rebecca opened the drain and watch the water swirl down. She'd clean the petal and leaf remnants out later. For now, she felt too good. She was going to stretch out on the bed and take a long, much needed nap.

***

The coyote led her through the familiar landscape. She saw the pond where she and Jerry had caught perch and bass their first summer here. She saw the blackberry bushes, laden with dark fruit. "Pick some," said the coyote. "Nothing as sweet as a fresh blackberry, warmed in the sun."

"I thought coyotes ate meat," Rebecca said.

"I'm not your normal coyote."

Rebecca plucked a blackberry from the bush, careful to avoid the thorns. It was warm and sweet like a blackberry pie fresh out of the oven.

"Jerry used to pick blackberries by the pail full. We'd never see most of them though. He'd eat them before he got them home."

"You know Jerry?"

"Jerry's an ornery sort. Especially once he gets something in his head. But then you know that. You've known him 'bout as long as anyone."

"You're his father. He recognized you in the painting."

"Good to see a son still knows his father." The coyote paused for a moment, then ran to the top of a rock ledge covered in pale green lichen. "He was king of this rock," the coyote howled. "Remind him."

And then he was gone.

Rebecca walked back home along the path, past the cedar grove, the pine grove, and the old Indian grave hidden in a field of daffodils. It was exactly as she

*remembered it that first day Easter Sunday when they'd
come to Jerry's mother's house for dinner. Jerry had taken
her hand and led her down the path. He'd proposed to her
right by the side of the Indian grave, surrounded by yellow
daffodils, white dogwoods, and the brilliant blue sky.*

Rebecca felt coolness against her neck and opened her
eyes. Jerry stood over her, holding a single white rose.
"Let's go to dinner," he said.

****

When Jerry took the highway down past Farmington and
into wine country, Rebecca knew it was more than just
going out to dinner. The only restaurant down that way was
Tiger Ridge, the posh new establishment they went to only
on special occasions. Excitement and trepidation mingled
as they stepped into the lobby. The blonde hostess greeted
them.

"Two for Evans," he said.

"Of course, Mr. Evans. This way." She led them into the
public dining area. A huge bison head hung on the wall, its
eyes still sorrowful and proud. They took a seat at a private
booth for two.

The waiter approached immediately, "Can I get you
something to drink?"

"Glen Fiddich on the rocks," Jerry said.

"12 year, 14 year, or 25 year?"

"25 year."

"Very well, sir," the waiter scribbled on the pad. "And
for you ma'am?"

Rebecca eyed her husband curiously, "I'll have the
same."

189

"I'll be right back with your drinks," the waiter said.

"What's the occasion?" Rebecca asked eager to end the suspense.

"I want to propose something to you," Jerry said.

"We're already married," Rebecca laughed. "Although it's funny you should mention a proposal."

"Why?" Jerry's eyes darted around uncomfortably.

Rebecca smiled. "When you woke me up, I was dreaming of the day you proposed to me. Do you remember?"

Jerry relaxed noticeably, "Of course I remember. It was right next to that Indian tomb."

"Exactly. There were daffodils and dogwoods all around. And it was Easter."

"I was so afraid you wouldn't say yes."

"Why?"

"Because I thought I didn't deserve you."

"Well, I did say yes."

"Yes, you did," Jerry reached out for her hand. "I'm so glad you did."

The waiter put their drinks on the table. Both sipped appreciatively. Rebecca could never get over the difference a few extra years in the barrel made when aging scotch. "Can I get you an appetizer?" the waiter asked.

Jerry glanced at the menu, "Smoked salmon with sherried cream cheese and chives alright, Becca?"

"Wonderful."

"Very well, sir." The waiter disappeared.

"You know, Becca, you are still so beautiful."

"Candlelight does wonders for a person," Rebecca touched her face tenderly. "Especially a bruised person."

"They're not so bad tonight."

"You could have fooled me," she sipped her scotch.

"I know. You still must hurt."

"Some. The bath helped."

"That's good," Jerry swirled the ice around in his glass and took another sip. "Anyway, about the proposal. I don't want you to say anything until I've finished. Agreed?"

"Agreed."

"I've had an offer for the back half of the land. Just the part from the pond to the green rocks – you know, the part we haven't walked on for years. It's a very good offer. Enough to retire on and live very well."

"We already live very well."

"Now hear me out," Jerry said. "You promised."

Rebecca nodded and sipped her scotch.

"Remember how we always said we'd travel? This would give us enough money to do that. Now, while we're still young. We wouldn't have to work twenty-five more years. We could retire now."

"I thought you liked your job."

"I do," Jerry motioned to the waiter for another scotch. "And I'd still work. Just not as often."

"I don't want to argue about this, Jerry." Rebecca finished her drink. "Let's just enjoy dinner. Tomorrow, we'll walk out on the land, like we used to and make our decision then."

Jerry looked at her strangely, "You're sure you're up to the hike?"

"I will be tomorrow," she swirled the ice in her glass.

He leaned over and kissed her, "I love you, Becca."

"I love you too," she whispered.

***

They made love again that night, and after Jerry fell asleep Rebecca went back to her canvases. This time she chose pastels. Chalk after chalk, blending the yellows and the whites, and the pale spring greens. When the morning dawned, cloudy and cold, her canvas greeted it with brown tree trunks arching upwards into white dogwood flowers, pierced with dark red, splayed out against the brilliant blue sky, daffodils blooming bright yellow amidst bright white bones. Two intertwined hands, one large and one small rested over the stepped burial mound. A gold ring circled the ring finger on each. Rebecca surveyed her work. It was softer than she'd meant it to be, but it was fitting somehow. "Forever Ours," she wrote onto a small piece of paper and propped it up beside her work.

Rebecca looked out the window at the season's first hard frost. The blades of grass shone white and hard against the grey morning, an old man's Mohawk shimmering in defiance. "Not the best day for a picnic," she sighed, preparing her muscles for the cold. The coyote stared back at her, insistent. "We'll go. Of course we'll go."

She went to the kitchen to start the coffee, surprised to see it burbling away. Jerry sat at the table, spreading cream cheese on toasted bagels. "I thought we might need a little sustenance before our journey."

"Like we didn't eat enough last night," she picked half a bagel off the plate.

"Well, I for one worked it off," he reached out for her other hand. "And judging by the colors on your hand, you worked all night again. You sure you're up for the walk."

"Never better," she said. "After coffee of course."

"Of course."

They drank two cups of coffee each, then went to the bedroom to change into warmer clothes. At last, they started out into the woods. Tuxedo and Hooch took off ahead of them, circling back occasionally to make sure their people were still following. As they hiked, they reminisced about other times they'd walked together through the woods. They passed the blackberry brambles, leaves turned brown and fallen to the ground, and remembered the years they'd braved ticks and heat and electrical storms to gather blackberries for the perfect jam.

At the bottom of the hill, they stopped briefly at the pond and talked about the fish they'd caught and those that got away – fish of legend who still swam along beneath the weeds. Jerry told of how his father had caught a snapping turtle one year and boiled it up for soup. He told of how he'd caught a duck as a young boy and his father had pried the hook from the duck's bill and set it flying free above the trees.

It started to snow. They left the pond and walked up the trail past the old lean-to, past the cedars, and to the Indian grave where they'd become engaged. The snow coated the twigs that surrounded the burial mound, making them look almost like bones. They kissed again upon the mound, as they had many years before. "Ready to go back?" Jerry asked.

"Not yet," Rebecca pulled him onward. "Let's go to the rocks."

"The rocks?" Jerry asked.

"The green rocks where you were King."

Jerry smiled and started forward, "I told you about that?"

"In a way," Rebecca answered.

"It was a pretty funny story. See, when I was younger there were boys who wanted to fight me. And so I brought them here. I told them if they could climb to the top of the green hill before I could that I'd fight them. The funny thing was, I always beat them. None of them knew how to walk on the slippery rock. So I was King on that rock."

"And you still are," Rebecca leaned over and kissed him. "Don't you see?"

"What?"

"There are too many memories here. They're worth more than early retirement."

"But Becca, memories are here," he stroked her head, "We don't need the land to keep them."

But you do.

"Did you say something?" Jerry looked over at Rebecca.

"No. But I heard something."

"Probably the wind."

"Probably."

They had reached the green rocks, now white with snow. "I've never seen them in the winter," Rebecca said.

"Oh, I have," Jerry smiled. "You think they're hard to climb when they're dry. Imagine now."

AAuuuAuuuAuuuu.

They both looked up to the pinnacle of the rocks. A sole coyote sat, howling at the sky. "Blind coyote," Jerry whispered. "Dad."

"How do you know?" Rebecca asked.

"I recognize his howl," Jerry said. "When I was young, we'd play Coyote and the Leaf Man." Jerry stopped suddenly.

"What's wrong?"

"I am the Leaf Man."

"What do you mean?"

"A patient yesterday…never mind…Becca, we're not selling the land. Not now and not ever. This land belongs to my father. And look, he's not alone."

Rebecca looked up and saw the man who'd haunted her paintings standing next to the coyote on the rock. "Running with Dogs," she murmured.

"That's right," Jerry put his arm around his wife. "How did you know his name?"

"Lucky guess," she answered, as Tuxedo and Hooch bounded down the hill toward them, snow clinging to their coats.

Jerry pulled Rebecca to him and they held each other close, letting the snow fall all around them as they inhaled each others' scent. When they finally looked up to the pinnacle of rock, both the coyote and his companion were gone.

The Protectors

By Rachelle Reese

Sylvia

The heat shimmered over the rows of tomatoes, peppers, and beans. "It really needs weeded," Sylvia told herself. But she was too hot to do it. As a younger woman, she would have waited until evening. Now in her eighties, she would most likely end up paying someone to do it.

She looked at the bright blue sky and prayed for rain, then lifted the pump handle of the well and watched the water jet upward from the sprinklers. The lawn soaked it up thankfully. She'd come out after the sun was lower to move the sprinklers to the vegetable garden. For now, she'd pick some vegetables for dinner.

"What are *you* doing there?" she asked, eyeing the long green hornworm in the tomatoes. "Sorry, but you're going to be duck food today." Sylvia plucked the worm from the nearly bare stem, wincing as it wriggled against her hand, just sticky enough to make its touch uncomfortable. She held the worm out and called for the ducks. Frasier waddled forward and snatched the worm from her fingers. Several other ducks gathered around to try to take the worm away. Frasier gobbled it hungrily before they could snatch it. "Your fault for being slow," Sylvia scolded. "You know what they say about the early bird."

Sylvia went back to her tomato plants, picking a few ripe tomatoes and holding them in her oversized t-shirt. She'd have tomatoes and beans for dinner tonight, she decided and walked toward the beans. As she reached toward the vine, she felt a pain burn heavy in her chest. "Maybe my time has come at last," she thought, but knew that wasn't it. The coyote's howl confirmed her fears. Another soul had passed before rising. Another protector had been taken. A cold hand tore at Sylvia's chest. Another howl, and then another. Birds screeched mercilessly. The ducks were in an uproar. In that moment, Sylvia knew the death had not been kind. The soul had not been freed.

Joanne

Joanne rushed out the door of her office building. She was already nearly half an hour late picking up her daughter Deborah at school. Luckily she'd been able to reach her friend Matt on his cell phone and he had agreed to pick Deborah up and take her home. At twelve, Deborah often protested that she was too old for a babysitter. Joanne figured this was as good a test as any. Still, she was anxious to get home. Tonight was the band concert at Deborah's school and Deborah had a solo on the clarinet. Joanne pulled onto the freeway and cursed. Wouldn't you know it, bumper to bumper. Probably an accident up ahead. Joanne pushed the relaxation CD she'd bought after she found out she was pregnant. Something else she still needed to tell Matt. Joanne pushed the thought out of her mind and concentrated on her breathing.

Sylvia

Sylvia opened her eyes and stared up at the blue sky. A single hawk circled. Everything was silent. How long had she been unconscious? She checked the position of the sun. It was sinking, but not much lower than it had been when the first coyote howled. Perhaps there was still time. She gathered her strength, knowing transformation would take everything she had. "Wait for me," she called to the hawk. Then she willed her skin to take another form. She felt her arms twist into wings and her skin prickle sharply as feathers sprouted from the hair follicles. The pain was almost unbearable as her arthritic legs shrank down to spindly bird legs. She cried out.

The hawk stopped circling and swooped down to the ground to join her, grooming her newly sprouted wings, soothing her pain. "You'll always love me, won't you?" Sylvia asked, amazed once again at the sounds she made. The hawk continued grooming her furiously. "I know. We don't have much time. Let's fly." They lifted off the ground at the same time and soared up into the deepening blueness of the sky, seeking the struggling soul.

The Soul

It knew only pain from the moment it awoke – more than the physical pain of the body that housed it. A spiritual pain like the skin being stripped from around a segment of

198

an orange and each juicy morsel smashed, pointlessly, under a relentless blade. Then finally, it stopped, leaving a dull ache. The soul felt the body's anger weaken – the anger that had been strong enough to wake the soul from its long slumber. The racing heartbeat slowed, then stopped. The body let out a final breath and on that breath the soul rode headlong into the darkness, carrying with it the only emotions it had ever known. Anger, bewilderment, and pain.

Joanne

Joanne pulled off the freeway just as the relaxation CD ended. Almost an hour to get down the freeway, she thought to herself, and for no good reason that she could see. She sped down the side roads and pulled into her driveway at last. She glanced at the clock. Nearly 6:30. It would be a real rush to get to the concert in time. She hurried up the walkway and opened the front door.

"Deborah, I'm home," she called.

No one answered. Joanne figured she probably had her music on or was in the shower and rushed up the stairs. When she reached the top, she heard nothing. "Deborah?" she called again. Still no answer. Joanne dialed Matt's cell phone number and got his voice mail. "Matt? Did you pick up Deborah? Call me." She hung up the phone and rushed from room to room, calling her daughter's name. No response.

Joanne went back to Deborah's room. The clarinet case lay on the bed. Had Deborah taken it with her this morning? Joanne couldn't remember. She dialed Matt's cell phone again. Voice mail. She looked again at the clarinet case on the bed. Maybe Matt had taken Deborah directly to the concert and forgotten the clarinet. She picked up the clarinet and headed to the car.

Breathe, the soul exhaled, feeling a rush when the leaves quivered on the tree branches. "I made that happen," it thought. *Breathe*. A silky voice spoke up from deep within the soul's dreams. *Breathe in as if you were the wind preparing to blow a storm cloud over a mountain.* The soul inhaled and felt its anger sucked inward. It spit it out, ripping a branch from the quivering tree. The tree screamed in anger and pain. The tree's scream felt good to the soul. "I made that happen," the soul thought. The soul inhaled again. This time deeper, feeling the anger fill it, stretch it. It focused on a different tree and released the pain, snapping another branch. Again it inhaled, but this time it let the air carry it skyward. It hovered over the trees, just beneath the clouds. "Feel my pain," it roared, exhaling its wrath into the forest, letting the force carry it spiraling down amongst the trees. A scream rose up from a young tree, its five-year roots yanked from the soil by the gust of wind. The youngster's agony joined the agony of the soul and made it stronger. This time the soul rose higher and exhaled with more force, taking a tree older and stronger than the one before it. The soul moved over the forest, devouring tree after tree, letting their anger and pain nurture its growth. *Breathe.* When the soul inhaled now, it drew the clouds together with its force. When it exhaled, the clouds knocked against each other, lightning bolts flashing between them. The soul was exhilarated by its power. Frenzied, it danced up the ridge and down into the valley, up the ridge and down into the valley, leaving behind a trail of trees wrenched from the ground. It no longer bothered to take the souls of the trees, leaving them scattered in broken pieces on the forest floor or trapped within the twisted trunks of the trees they once inhabited. At last, the soul grew tired and rested on a hillside. The soul felt drops of water weeping from the clouds, washing away the crimson streams it had seen on its body's thighs in the moment it awoke, turning them clear and pure. The soul closed its eyes and remembered music. *Flight of the Bumblebee*. It knew in that moment where home was.

Sylvia

Sylvia looked at the handsome hawk flying by her side. Jake. They had been lovers long ago, when their protector souls were beginning to awaken. It was almost as if each had recognized the kindred soul hidden inside the other. They met in 1942 and Sylvia can still remember the day she saw the boy lying by the side of the road in Litzmannstadt Ghetto.

"I am drabengi," she said in her native tongue. His emaciated body barely moved when she touched his shoulder. He didn't answer. *Save him*, a voice spoke over her shoulder. She turned and there was no one there. She turned back to the boy. Large brown wings had encircled his body, feathers ruffled as if to keep him warm. They were the wings of a hawk. *Save him for me.*

She knew the fever. It was like the one that had killed her husband a year before. She had not been able to heal her husband, but now she needed to save this boy. She lifted the boy in her arms and took him into her home, frightened by his weightlessness. Carefully, she prepared the herbs, grown covertly in the window of her cramped apartment. She looked at the boy's chiseled dark skin and wondered if he was Roma like her or a Jew. Not that it mattered much to her. The hawk had told her to save him and that's what she would do. She sprinkled the herbs over the boy's body and rubbed a bit of healing oil into his temples. Then she called on the goddess to save this boy's life.

All night, she watched the boy. Finally, as the fingers of dawn pulled the sun over the edge of her windowsill, the boy opened his eyes. "Good morning," she said in her own language, wondering if he'd understand.

"Who are you?" he replied in German. "An angel?"

"I am Sylvia," she spoke in German, giving him her Christian name. She and her husband had both taken a Christian baptism shortly after they were married. They had moved to a new town and hoped to escape the persecution that had left her mother, father, and baby sister murdered in their beds. "I found you lying in the street and brought you here."

"Thank you," he said. "My name is Jacob."

Jewish, she thought, *what would he think when he found out she was Roma?* "You had a high fever, Jacob. I brought you here to heal you."

"Are you a nurse?" he asked.

"I am a healer. My people call me a drabengi."

"Your people? You are not Jewish?"

"No. I am Roma."

"I thought only Jewish people lived here."

"There are a small group of us Roma left. There were more once. The Nazis have been taking us away train by train."

"What do they do with you?"

"They kill us. That's what I've heard."

"Do they kill us too?" Jacob's eyes looked fearful. "When they take us away, do they kill us?"

Sylvia knew the look. She'd seen it in her own eyes and the eyes of those around her too many times not to recognize it in this stranger's eyes. "Who did they take?"

"My parents," Jacob whispered.

Sylvia wrapped her arms around the skinny boy as the hawk had wrapped his wings. "Let's hope the rumors are wrong."

Jake

Jake watched the graceful jet black raven glide next to him. After all these years, she was still beautiful to him – as a raven and as a woman. He remembered the first time she had become the raven. He was in her small apartment in the ghetto. His body had become strong again and they both knew he would live. He also knew that he was in love with her, but he hadn't told her, afraid that she would think him too young to be serious.

The Gestapo had opened her front door and yelled in German, "Gypsy! Come with us. You're going to a new place."

Jake had watched, amazed as the beautiful dark haired woman disappeared and a sleek black raven took her place in the center of her multicolored skirts, and then flew out the open door above the heads of the three Gestapo officers. They did not seem to notice the bird's departure.

"No gypsy here," Jacob had called out, trying not to let fear cause his voice to tremble.

"Where is she?" one of the officers asked, shining a light under Jacob's chin.

"Gone," Jacob held his gaze steady. "I never met her."

Another officer held up a bright blue ankle-length skirt. "Then I suppose this skirt is yours, pretty boy?" The other officers laughed.

"I'm just looking for food," Jacob whispered. "I'm starving."

"Get a job," the officer knocked his chin roughly, but pulled the light away. "The only good Jew is a working Jew."

"The only good Jew is a dead Jew," a short burly officer whispered behind Jacob, causing a shiver to run up his spine.

"Not tonight, Heinrich. Tonight's train is for the gypsies."

The short burly officer grunted and the three Gestapo left, leaving the door open to the cold behind them.

It was many days before Sylvia returned, her black feathers beating against the closed window. She told him later that she had waited in the trees and followed the train. She wanted to know where they were taking her friends. She described the death camp vaguely at first, then later in more detail. Each time she talked of the death camps, he thought of his mother and father and wondered if their deaths had been painful.

Sylvia

Sylvia heard the scream of a tree spirit, wrenched from its tree and thrown to the ground. *We're too late*, she thought. *It's awakened and angry.* In all the years she'd watched for new protectors, she'd dealt with only one that had been disembodied at the moment of its awakening. And she, her own soul newborn as the raven, had not known what to do.

It was at the death camp. A very young Roma boy – seven at most – had been taken to the gas chamber blindfolded. A protector spirit waited within the boy. As the gas caused the body to convulse, the spirit was ejected. After the boy fell dead on the concrete floor, the soul, in the form of a bear, gathered the body into his arms and paced up and down the chamber. When the door opened, the bear-soul placed the boy's body on the ground, and lunged at the entrant, ripping his heart from his chest. The bear went on to kill many Gestapo that night and many Roma. It didn't know its victims or their crimes. It only felt anger at the death of its boy-body. Sylvia had watched powerless. As the Romas died, she flew alongside their souls as far as she could fly, trying to explain what she herself didn't understand. She assured them that their death was not caused by their own impurity, but that of the Gestapo. It was all she could do.

Now, she looked down on tree-spirits lying broken on the ground and knew her task. She motioned for Jake to go on and look for the lost protector, then soared down to wake and guide each spirit home.

Jake

Jake followed the wind up and down the valleys, watching it rip spirits from the earth and throw their remains onto the ground. "Protector," he called. "Hear me. I can help."

The wind-soul did not answer his cries.

He flew faster, toward the painful screams. Up and down the sides of the ravine he raced until he felt the violent wind lift his wings and hurl him into a rock. He felt pain in his shoulder and knew his wing was injured. He hobbled to a nearby crevice to hide from the angry wind and assess the damage. He wondered whether Sylvia knew.

She always seemed to know when he was hurt. She had always known a lot about him.

She'd known about the hawk soul. He hadn't believed her. "Will yourself to grow feathers and you will," she'd coaxed. "We can fly out of here."

"I don't know your witchcraft, Sylvia. And I can't learn."

"It's not witchcraft, Jake." She took his hand and put it on her arm. "Feel me while I do it." He felt feathers sprout as her arms contorted into wings.

He tried to will feathers to sprout on his arms. Nothing happened. "It's no use, Sylvia. We'll have to figure out another way."

"There is no other way," she sighed.

"You go without me then," he'd been worried that they'd come for her again. There were only a few Roma left in the ghetto.

"I won't leave you, Jake."

And she didn't leave. Together, they stayed in hiding. When they heard the Gestapo approach, Sylvia took the shape of a raven and flew out the window. But one night her change was slow. One of the officers saw it happen and yelled, "Grab the crow! The gypsy is a witch."

Another officer threw his coat over her, trapping her.

Jake remembered nothing of the change, except that suddenly he was rushing at the officer who had Sylvia trapped, wings spread full. He tore out the officer's eyes, grabbing them with his beak. The other officer tried to shoot, but missed as Jake swooped down and picked up the coat, freeing Sylvia. The two of them flew together out the open door, over the ghetto walls, and into the country. Jake could not remember feeling so free – maybe as a young child. He breathed the fresh air and felt the wind rush under his wings.

The two of them flew to a place far outside the ghetto. *The trees will provide cover*, he understood Sylvia's caw. They swooped down and roosted on the branch of an oak tree. "Can you sleep on your feet in bird form?" Sylvia asked.

"I don't know," he replied. "I've never done it before."

Sylvia chuckled and took her perch, "You'll learn."

And he had learned, preferring even to this day to sleep on his feet in bird form when he sensed an enemy.

Sylvia

She knew Jake was hurt. She always knew the moment it happened, ever since the first time she saw the hawk's wings wrapped around him. She also knew that it would take both of them to reign in this soul. As she grew closer, she felt what had happened to the soul and the body it was meant to live in. She felt its pain and sorrow. She also knew its cause – not from the soul because it didn't know, but from the other spirits around her. She was near where it had happened and she saw the residue of death and lust crawling on the ground beneath her. The spirits around the site cowered. She knew they needed comfort, but there wasn't time. The soul was airborne and confused.

Sylvia soared upwards and flew as fast as she could toward Jake. She would soothe his pain and they would fly together, as they had flown the first night he changed and many nights after that as they fled into the northern forests. She remembered the first night they made love. An ice storm had driven them into a cave, their wings glistening, their feathers frozen solid. She had groomed him, nibbling

207

the ice from his feathers until he was fluffed up and warm. She had shown him how to do the same for her. Survival. That was all it was. But when his beak caressed her under her pin feathers, she felt a thrill. She realized that she had loved him all this time. "Let's shift back to human," she whispered. "I want to hold you as a man."

"How?" he asked.

"Just will it," she said. And so they became man and woman again. They held each other close and felt flesh meld to flesh. He caressed her neck and breasts with his mouth. She caressed his nipples and his thighs with hers. Then shivering, as much from passion as from cold, they came together. It was the first time Jake had entered a woman and Sylvia had guided him patiently. She was, after all, an experienced woman of eighteen. And he was…she remembered she didn't really know his age. She had thought of him as a boy when she'd found him. Now, as she stroked his body, she realized that he was not a boy, but a man.

"Sixteen," he said, as if reading her mind. "I turned sixteen not long before you found me."

She laughed and pulled him deeper inside her. She had been only twelve on her wedding night and her husband had been twenty-two. It was the Roma way. "No guilt," she said.

"What is guilt?" he replied. "I love you Sylvia."

"Jacob," she gasped, feeling him press against her insides.

"Sylvia," he sighed. And there was no more talk.

Jake felt the raven coming before he saw her, felt the urgency in her flight. *She's seen something I haven't.* And then he saw her coming toward him, a branch of some herb clutched in her beak. And above her, a murder of crows flew toward the hills she'd left behind.

Sylvia landed next to him and immediately began shredding the herb branch into strands and weaving it between the feathers.

"Will I be able to fly?" he asked.

"Let's hope," she muttered. "Of all the times to hurt yourself."

"It was the wind," he explained.

"It was the soul. The soul's form is the wind." She finished weaving the herb and chirped a few words in her native tongue.

Jake had never tried to understand her rituals. He only knew his wing felt better. "I think I can fly."

"Good. We'll have to fly fast to catch the wind."

"Which direction?" Jake asked.

"Which way did the wind throw you?"

Jake moved his head to simulate the wind throwing him against the rock.

"Then we'll go..." Sylvia started to motion in one direction, but then she heard it. And Jake heard it also. Music. Both of them took to the air, following *The Flight of the Bumblebee*.

Joanne

Joanne arrived at the school auditorium and heard the familiar strains of one of the marching songs Deborah had practiced relentlessly over the past several months. She was glad her daughter had such a passion for music and she was proud of her accomplishments, but some days she just needed silence. It hadn't been so bad the last few weeks. Deborah had learned the songs almost perfectly, rarely stumbling over the notes even when the notes came quickly, as they did in the solo she was playing tonight. Joanne hoped she wasn't too late and crept silently into the darkened auditorium, finding a seat at the back. She strained to find her daughter on the stage, but couldn't see her. A chill ran through her as she noticed that the first clarinet chair sat empty.

Sylvia

They flew together out of the woods and down tree-lined suburban streets, following the music. Several times it became faint with distance, but they always managed to find it again. Sylvia was not familiar with the suburbs, preferring to live as far away from people as she could. She relied on Jake to navigate their path between buildings and over six-foot privacy fences. If people thought it odd to see a raven and a hawk flying together, Sylvia didn't notice.

At last she heard the music growing louder. *We must have closed the distance.* Rustic Hills Middle School, she read the sign. Not so rustic from the looks of things, she grimaced. And then she felt the soul. Still whistling the song, it beat against the walls of the building. *It doesn't know how to get in.* She flew to a nearby tree and landed on a branch. Jake landed next to her. It was a young tree, unaccustomed to the weight of two large birds. It moaned a little under their weight. "Patience," Sylvia coaxed. "We won't be long."

"Why do you think it wants to get in the auditorium?" Jake asked.

"I'm not sure. Maybe there's something in there it wants."

Jake and Sylvia watched the front door of the auditorium open as a man stepped inside. As the door opened they heard the strident sounds of an amateur band rush outward. When it closed, there was silence. "It followed him in," Sylvia said.

"What now?" Jake asked. "Two birds can't just fly into a school auditorium."

Sylvia considered their options. There were too many people around to shift back into human form right here. And if they left, the soul might leave unnoticed. She thought of the bear-soul in the death camp and the tree-spirits lying broken on the ground. "We risk it," she flew to a shadowy spot between two buildings.

Jake took her meaning and followed. "We'll be naked," he said as he landed beside her. "We can't just walk into a school auditorium naked." He noticed her feathers had already started to retract.

"What then? We can't just let it...."

"I know," Jake paced back and forth. "Maybe someone else will go inside and we can follow."

Sylvia nodded and Jake saw her feathers grow back shiny and black. The two birds stood outside the auditorium and watched the door.

Matt

Matt felt a warm breeze wash over and past him as he stepped into the auditorium. He hurried down the hall and slipped into the darkened auditorium, taking a seat toward the back. He'd forgotten his glasses and now his eyes strained to make out Joanne's little girl sitting in the clarinet section. He wasn't sure, but he thought he saw her. Relieved, he sat back to listen to the music.

Joanne

Joanne slipped out of her seat and into the hallway. Maybe they didn't have a spare clarinet for Deborah, she reasoned. She's probably backstage wondering where I am with her clarinet. Joanne rushed down the empty hall to the backstage door. As she neared it, she heard the familiar strains of Deborah's solo. *The Flight of the Bumblebee.* That was what it was called. She felt relief flood over her as she stepped into the backstage door, clarinet clutched tightly in her hand.

"Deborah?" a voice whispered through the dark. "Thank god you're here. It's almost time for your solo."

Jake

Jake heard a car pull up along the sidewalk, just past the parking lot. Something about the driver made him uneasy. *Predator*, the voice that sometimes spoke to him growled. *Prey.* Jake took to the air to get a closer look.

"Where are you going?" Sylvia cawed.

Jake didn't answer.

Sylvia watched the hawk approach a car parked with its lights out. Her sharp bird eyes saw the flash of fire and then the amber glow of a lit cigarette. She saw the hawk perch in a tree and watch, just for a moment, then fly back toward her.

"Do you think he's going in?" Sylvia asked.

"Let's hope not," Jake answered. "Unfortunately, he's not mine."

"What do you mean, not yours?"

"This one belongs to the wind."

Sylvia nodded, remembering what the spirits had shown her. Remembering the residue of death. "You'll need to teach it."

Jake looked at her solemnly, "Let's hope it's a fast learner."

"I'll be there just in case," Sylvia said sadly.

"I hope it doesn't come to that," Jake looked over at the car bitterly. "I won't let it come to that."

Matt

Matt opened his eyes as he heard the first few bars of Deborah's solo. He'd drifted off to sleep, as he always did in dark places with bad music, but he'd know that solo anywhere. *Flight of the Bumblebee.* He'd heard her practice it enough. He blinked the sand out of his eyes so that he could watch her play. He strained to see the stage. No little girl stood playing the solo. The music just floated through the air, wafted side to side and all around. Nice trick for a middle school concert, he thought. When it was over, the audience applauded and he could swear he felt a warm breeze brush against his cheek. And then it was gone.

The Soul

The soul heard the applause and breathed in a new emotion – happiness. The people-spirits were happy. They

213

loved the music. The soul whipped around the room, brushing up against the faces of the people it knew – the people she knew. They would be sad when they found out what had happened to the body, to her, to me. The soul remembered all these people and the music just like the girl had known him. *Just like I had known them.* The soul hovered near her best friend and saw the sheet music flutter and fall to the ground. *I did that. Sorry Beth.* The soul knew her name and knew she didn't have a mother or a father in the audience. They were both too busy to watch her play. The soul also knew Beth would be walking home alone. *I will protect you, Beth*, the soul whispered and watched her friend pick up her sheet music. The soul sat amongst her friends and played the songs they'd learned together.

When they'd played the last song, the audience applauded and once again the soul felt happy. When she bowed, sheet music fluttered all around and her friends giggled and scrambled to pick it up. She followed her friends backstage and saw her mother waiting in the wings. She rushed toward her to kiss her and then remembered she had no body, only air. She blew against her mother's cheek gently. "I'm alright," she whispered. "I remember you now and I won't leave you."

Her mother looked around frantically and called, "Deborah!"

The soul remembered that was her name and realized her mother couldn't hear her. The soul felt lonely and helpless.

Jake

Jake saw the dark-haired girl walking alone toward the car. He saw the cigarette tip move over to the passenger side window and the girl got in. "Let's go," he said.

214

Sylvia nodded and took flight behind him. "We need to find the wind," she called.

"I'll follow him. You find the wind."

Sylvia could feel the wind-soul still inside the auditorium. She waited for the door to open and swooped inside, narrowly missing a woman's hair. The woman screamed. Sylvia chattered an apology and flew along the hallway to the backstage door. She sensed the soul inside and knew its sorrow. "Come with me, wind-soul. You can console her later."

The wind-soul blew around the room, as if looking for the voice.

"Here. I'm the raven."

"You can see me?" the wind-soul asked.

"I can sense you. I'll explain later. For now, we need to teach you what you are."

"What am I?"

"A protector. And there's a girl who needs your protection."

Sylvia could feel the wind-soul grow cold, "Beth!"

The wind-soul flew out the door, carrying Sylvia with it. Down the hall, they flew together, oblivious to shock of the people still mingling in the halls. The wind-soul seemed to know its way and on they flew out the door of the building, down the road, around one corner and then another until finally Sylvia saw Jake and the car up ahead. Wind and wings, they chased after the car until the wind overtook it. "Careful," Sylvia cautioned. "Your friend is inside."

"I know," the soul cried out. "What do I do?"

"Just follow for now."

215

"He'll kill her," the soul screamed. "He'll do things to her and kill her. Like he did Deborah...like he did me."

"You'll stop him before that. Or Jake will."

"Jake?"

"The hawk. He's a protector like you."

Beth

Beth knew she'd made a mistake as soon as the man turned onto the highway. Maybe she knew it before, when she'd seen his lips curl around the cigarette, when she'd seen his eyes glance down at her black velvet thigh. Now she shrank against the passenger door, just out of reach of his hand. She'd already decided to make a run for it if he stopped at a light. If. What if he didn't? What then?

The car turned off the highway onto a gravel road.

"Comfortable?" the man asked.

Beth nodded, not sure what else to do.

"Too bad. I prefer it when they squirm." The man ground his cigarette into the ashtray and lit another. "Think about that on your thigh."

Beth crossed her legs and scrunched closer against the door. She wondered if she'd die if she just opened the door and rolled out of the car and onto the gravel. She was sure it would hurt, but not as much as a cigarette burn. Not as much as what she knew he meant to do.

On and on they drove. She watched the house lights get further and further apart until she couldn't remember how far back the last house was. Still they drove. She watched the wind whip through the treetops, trying to keep her mind off the man and what he might do. She watched a hawk sail by outside her window. And another smaller black bird –

crow? raven? She was never too good at telling the two apart.

Finally, the man pulled the car onto a road and stopped. She grabbed for the handle, but he was faster. He held her wrist tight with his hand and yanked her across the front seat and out the driver's door. He held her hands over her head and bent her over the hood of the car, grinding against her backside. She tried to get away, then realized he had snapped handcuffs around her wrists and slipped a noose over her neck.

"One false move and you hang," he growled. "Now come with me." He pushed her down the hill.

Beth heard crows cawing beneath her. Crows, not ravens. She was sure of that now. She saw them clutching the skinned limbs of bodies hung from trees. Young girl bodies like her own. Beth screamed.

The man clasped his hand over her mouth. "Want to be like them, keep screaming," he growled, his voice breathy. He reached his hand around her and pushed his hand down inside her pants.

Beth heard the wind stir up around them, flinging the treetops in circles. She felt wings flapping overhead. Crows? Too large.

The Soul

"Can't hurt Beth," the soul screamed to those who could hear it. "Can't hurt Beth."

"I'll distract him," Jake cried and swooped down on the man, grasping his hair in his claws. The man's hands went up to his head and the girl ran. Jake kept hold of the man's hair and pecked at his ear.

217

The soul drew in hatred and anger. This was the man who'd killed Deborah. This was the man who'd hurt Beth and all the others hanging from the trees. The soul felt their anger fill her and rushed in on the man, lifting him off his feet. She felt twisted and swirling and the man swirled inside her until he puked. Finally she flung him outward, unwanted flesh hurling into a slab of rock. A hawk descended on him, plucking out his eyes, tearing at his flesh.

The soul sank back into the forest, looking for her friend, her Beth. She found her curled beneath the trees, a naked old lady cradling her head in her lap.

The Thaw

By Rachelle Reese

Tonight it started the way it always did. With snow. Large, crystalline flakes fluttering to the ground, sticking to her eyelashes, touching her lips. Melting at first and then sticking. Ice covered her hands and her face. Her jeans were stiff. She was immobile. That was when she'd wake up. Every time. Slowly, she'd move her fingers, then her mouth, and finally her eyelids. She'd find herself in bed, buried deep in the covers, but shivering. Tonight she couldn't warm up, even snuggled next to Kevin. She climbed out of bed and put on her terry cloth robe. Then she started to build a fire.

A fire could always drive away the dream. Something about watching the red coals flare up into blue and yellow flames when she breathed on them made her feel powerful.

Powerful enough to melt the ice. She'd been having the dream for as long as she could remember, which wasn't as long as most people her age could remember, but it was a long time. She stacked the wood carefully. Kindling cross-hatched to start. She'd add the log after the kindling caught fire. That was how she always did it. One time Kevin had asked her why and she'd answered, "Just because." The truth was, she didn't know why she built fires the way she did. She only knew she had always built them that way.

She lit a match and touched it to the shredded paper she'd stuffed beneath the kindling. An infant flame flickered, and then grew tall and wide. She watched it cautiously, praying it would light the kindling. It did. She watched the kindling burn a few moments, and then added a small split log. Then another. She sat in front of the fire, legs crossed Indian style and felt the heat creep through her blood, melting the ice, making her strong.

Eventually she went back to bed. Kevin rolled over and put his arm around her. "Dream again?" he asked.

"Mmmhmmm."

"I'm sorry."

"It's okay. I built a fire."

"I know," he kissed her forehead. "I can smell it."

Moments later, she heard Kevin snore. She felt the tiredness seep through her and let his soft snoring put her to sleep.

****

"What is your first memory?" Dr. Thomas asked. Kevin had convinced her to see a psychologist now that she had insurance that would cover it.

"Springtime," she answered. "Daffodils and mud."

220

"How old were you?"

"How old am I now?" She was beginning to think this was going to be a waste of time.

"Your file shows you are twenty-five."

"I was younger. I barely had breasts."

"So, would you say you were thirteen? Fourteen?"

"Sure," she started to stack pencils on the desk as if they were kindling.

"Why are you stacking the pencils like that?" Dr. Thomas eyed her curiously.

"It's just something I do."

"I see," Dr. Thomas scribbled something on her pad. "So you remember nothing before the time you were thirteen or fourteen?"

"Nothing significant. Nothing that tells me who I am."

"Tell me what you do remember."

"The song itsy-bitsy spider. And a soft knee. The woman who sang it with me had white hair and smelled like lilacs."

"Your grandmother?"

"I don't know."

"Anything else?"

"Smells."

"What kind of smells?"

"Bread baking, chocolate chip cookies, bacon frying, toast, other smells but I can't really identify them."

"Food seems very important to you," Dr. Thomas scribbled again.

"Food is very important to anyone who has starved." She looked at the doctor keenly. It was obvious Dr. Thomas hadn't missed too many meals lately.

"Then you remember being hungry."

"I remember it very well. When I stepped out of the cave, the sunlight hurt my eyes. And the yellow daffodils were so bright. But what I remember most about that day is the hunger."

"Okay. Let's start there. Tell me about that day."

"My jeans were torn and so loose I had to wrap a grapevine around my waist to keep them on. I knew I needed to eat something because my stomach hurt and I felt weak. The problem was, I didn't know what to eat. So I sat down outside the cave and watched. The first thing I saw was a bird -- a cardinal I know now. It was bright red. It poked its beak at the ground and brought up a worm. Then it slurped it down. Well, if birds can eat worms, maybe I can too, I thought. So I dug down in the ground and found a worm. And I ate it. It was cold when it went down my throat. Cold and slimy. But I ate another and another. Eventually I felt stronger and stood up to walk around and see what else I could find to eat."

"You ate worms?" Dr. Thomas looked at her incredulously over her reading glasses.

"Yes," she said simply. "And I'd do it again if I had to. What? Does that make me crazy?"

"No, of course not." Dr. Thomas scribbled again on her pad. "What else did you do that day?"

"I walked. I saw some deer grazing in a field. They were eating grass, so I tried that too. It was hard to chew, but I swallowed it anyway. Then I found some dandelions. I was wary at first because I'd tasted a daffodil and it was bitter, but the dandelions were surprisingly good."

"Daffodils are poisonous," Dr. Thomas noted.

"Well, I didn't eat much of it. In fact, I spit it out. It was very nasty. After tasting the daffodil, I decided that bees were not a very good judge of what was good to eat."

"At the time, did you know the words for deer, bee, bird, grass, worm?"

"Yes. I knew what most things were in a general way. I knew a bird was a bird, but I didn't know cardinal or blue jay."

"Didn't you wonder how you got there?"

"I couldn't remember being anywhere else."

"I see," Dr. Thomas scribbled some more. "So even on that day, you could not remember parents or where you had come from."

"Less than now. At that time, I remembered one thing."

"And what was that?"

"Fear."

Dr. Thomas looked at her curiously, and wrote the single word in big bold letters on her pad. The bell on the desk rang. Dr. Thomas looked at her watch. "I'm sorry, Carol. It looks like we'll have to pick this up next session."

"Doesn't seem like we accomplished much."

"Be patient. These things can take some time." Dr. Thomas pulled out her appointment book. "It looks like I

223

have a full hour open next week if you'd like a longer session."

Carol shook her head, "The insurance will only cover up to so much."

Dr. Thomas shrugged. "Alright. Next week then at the same time. Oh, and it might help if you start keeping a journal."

"What should I write?"

"Anything. Dreams, memories, the day's events."

"Sure," Carol was already half planning to cancel next week's appointment. She gathered her purse and walked out of the office.

****

Carol met Kevin for lunch at a restaurant near the greenhouse where she'd just started working as a botanist. They usually didn't see each other in the middle of the day, but today he'd scheduled appointments near the greenhouse because Carol had been nervous about talking to a psychologist. Carol was waiting at the table when he arrived.

Kevin kissed her and took the seat across from her. "So how did it go?"

"A complete waste of time," Carol sipped her iced tea. "I don't think I'll go back."

"It was that bad?" Kevin poured a packet of sugar into the iced tea she'd ordered for him. He liked his tea sweet. She liked hers black. That was only one of the many ways they were different, but for some reason they had fallen in love.

"She asked me how old I was when I stepped out of the cave."

"So?"

"So how would I know? It's the first thing I remember."

Kevin sipped his tea and added another sugar packet. "Okay. What else?"

Carol started to laugh. "She was shocked I'd eaten worms. You should have seen her face!" Carol mimicked Dr. Thomas and Kevin laughed with her.

"My shocking girl!" Kevin looked over the menu. "I see no worms on the menu. What do you want to eat?"

"One of everything!" Carol exclaimed. "She had me talking about food the whole time."

Kevin rolled his eyes. "Your eyes are bigger than your stomach. I'm getting the bacon cheeseburger and fries."

"I'll have the hot buffalo chicken sandwich and fries." Carol scowled at the menu. "Oh and let's get the artichoke dip as an appetizer."

"Sure, but you'll never eat all that."

"Wanna bet?"

"Loser gives the winner a massage."

"It's a bet!" Carol sipped on her tea.

Kevin motioned to the waitress that they were ready to order. She came over, pencil and pad in hand. As Kevin spoke, the waitress wrote with broad strokes on the pad.

Carol glanced at the pad as the waitress turned away.

FEAR

She'd written it in big, bold letters just like Dr. Thomas had. Carol blinked her eyes, but the waitress had turned the pad inward against her chest.

"What's wrong?" Kevin asked. "Did I order something wrong?"

"No....Excuse me." Carol got up and walked to the ladies room. She splashed cold water on her face and tried to convince herself she'd been mistaken. *Seeing things is more like it.* She looked in the mirror and was almost relieved to see herself looking back. She looked normal enough. If seeing a psychologist was going to make her crazy, she'd just stop going. It was that easy. One more splash of water. Carol dabbed her face dry with a rough paper hand towel. She rifled through her purse for some lipstick. Nothing. Oh well. *It's not like Kevin has never seen me without makeup.* She closed her purse and made her way back to the table.

"Everything alright?" Kevin asked.

"Fine." Carol sat down and reached for a chip. "But I've decided I'm definitely not going back."

"Okay," Kevin knew it was useless to argue with her.

Carol dipped a chip in the creamy cheese and artichoke dip and once again felt ravenous. She ate more than her share of the artichoke dip, finished her sandwich and fries, and still had room for a piece of cherry pie.

****

Carol stopped by the grocery store after work to get some things for dinner and some dog food for Gruff. Gruff had been with her almost from the beginning. She remembered the day she found him -- or more appropriately the day he found her. She'd happened upon a thicket of blackberries and was picking them hungrily, eating each one as she picked it. She'd seen a nice clump of blackberries inside a thorny mass of branches and she was trying to wedge her hand through. *Grrrr-rrufff!* she heard behind her and jumped, scraping her hand badly. *Grrrr-RRuff!* she turned around. There he was, a little black and white puff-ball. He fit in one hand. She picked him up and tried to feed him a blackberry. He spit it out. "Where'd you come from?" she asked. *Grrr-RRUFF!* he answered and licked her face. She'd laughed and put him on the ground. "Come on then. We'll find food together."

She had called him Gruff because that was the noise he made. And she'd tried to get him to eat everything she had eaten in the months she'd walked through these woods. He wouldn't eat any of it. Finally, they came upon a bag of corn, torn open for the deer. She'd seen the deer eat that and tried it herself, but the kernels were too hard for her to chew. She scooped some up in her hand and held it out for Gruff. He nuzzled it at first and looked up at her, cocking his head. "Go on, eat it," she said. He put his nose into her palm and began to eat. When he finished what was in her hand, he moved on to the bag. Finally full, he drank from a puddle of water and curled up in a ball in the sun. She scooped up what was left of the bag of corn and put it in the old sheet she'd tied up to carry the things she found. That day it held a slightly rusty pocket knife, a shiny white shoe too small for her foot, a glass jar without a lid, three bright-colored bugs with hooks sticking out of them, a frayed rope, a pack of not-too-soggy matches, and a hat. She didn't know why she'd kept these things, but thought she might have a use for them someday.

Gruff ate corn and caught an occasional mouse. She ate mostly blackberries until the sun dried them up. Most nights they slept beneath the stars. On rainy nights, they curled up together inside the cave. Gruff grew. One day, he proudly brought a squirrel to her. "Go ahead and eat it," she said. "I don't know what to do with it." He dropped it at her feet and whined, wagging his tail. She wasn't sure why, but she knew it would taste better cooked. She gathered up wood and stacked it cross-hatched. Then she stuffed some twigs and dry leaves beneath it and lit a match. She watched intently while the twigs and dry leaves burned and then the sticks caught fire. Gradually, she added bigger and bigger pieces of wood. The fire blazed. She looked from the fire to the squirrel. Now what? she wondered. Was there even any meat under all that hair? She found some large leaves and wrapped the squirrel in them, then put it on the red hot coals. She knew the leaves would just burn off if she set it in the flames. She left it there, listening to it sizzle. How would she know when it was done? Gruff sat next to her, sniffing the air. Then she could smell it too. It was a familiar smell, but all mixed up in her mind. It was pleasant, but frightening both at once. She grabbed a stick and pushed the leaf-wrapped squirrel off the coals. Gruff sniffed at it and let out a whelp. "Let it cool." Gruff backed away and sat back down next to her. He looked at the leaf-wrapped squirrel and whined. "Alright, I'll try it." She poked the leaf away with a stick. The smell of signed hair and skin made her gag. "I don't think I can eat it," she said. "But you're welcome to it. Just let it cool first." Gruff sniffed at the squirrel again and backed away. Several times, he nudged it. Then finally, he started to nibble at the singed fur. Before long he had torn the skin away to reveal meat. He started to eat. She'd crept closer and looked at what Gruff was eating so intently. It didn't look bad once the hair was gone. She tore off a small chunk and put it in her mouth. It didn't taste bad. She tore off another chunk. Together she and Gruff finished off that squirrel.

They ate better after that. Gruff would catch a squirrel now and then and she would roast it on the fire. He caught birds too and she learned that it was better to pluck their feathers before putting them on the fire.

Carol put a bag of dog food in the cart and grabbed a sack of rawhide bones. These days Gruff didn't hunt much -- well, still the occasional mouse. But mostly he'd gotten pretty lazy.

She continued walking down the aisle, adding milk to the cart, a bottle of chardonnay, chicken, provolone cheese, tri-colored rotini, a bag of spinach, a loaf of garlic bread. At the cash register, she glanced at the picture on the back of the milk carton as she put the milk on the conveyer belt. *Was my picture there once?* she wondered once again. She picked up a spiral bound notebook and a pen from the back-to-school display and put them on the conveyer belt too. Maybe she would try writing in a journal. What harm could it do? She'd start by writing down the story of Gruff.

****

"Why was the smell of the cooking squirrel frightening?" Dr. Thomas asked.

Carol had decided to give the psychologist one more try and had let her read the story of Gruff from the spiral-bound pages. "I don't know. It just was."

"Does the smell of cooking meat still frighten you?"

"Not the meat. It's the smell of singed hair that frightens me."

"Have you ever burnt your hair?"

"Not that I remember," Carol ran her hand through her short-cropped hair.

"Do fires frighten you?"

Carol laughed, "No. Fires make me strong."

"Let's go back to the word Fear. Last week you said that was all you remembered that spring. Can you describe the fear you remembered?"

"No." Carol started stacking pencils on the desk. "Let's talk about something else."

"What would you like to talk about?"

"I don't know. Just not that."

"Okay. Why don't you tell me how you became interested in ...." Dr. Thomas glanced down at her file "....botany."

"Well, it started in the woods, I guess. I learned that some plants were edible and others were not. Then when I worked with Javier and the others on the farm, I became interested in how to make plants grow better and provide better food."

"Who was Javier?"

Carol grinned, "You would have had a time analyzing Javier."

"Tell me about him."

"Javier was an old man when I met him, but he could pick vegetables faster than any of the younger workers. And all the time he picked, he talked about his wife and kids and grandkids back in Mexico. He was going back to see them in November. That's what he always did. Picked vegetables from June through October, then went back home for the winter. He didn't like the cold too much."

"How did you meet Javier?"

"Gruff met him first. It was hot and dry. The blackberries had all dried up and so had a lot of the other plants I'd been eating. Gruff was still catching squirrels and the occasional bird, but I was out of matches, so he was eating them by himself. Also, the creeks we'd been drinking from were mostly dry. What water there was tasted bad. We had walked far from the cave in search of something I could eat and fresh water to drink. As we walked over a hill, we saw a fence. And inside the fence there were plants. Rows and rows of plants, including corn. Gruff must have smelled the corn because he rushed down the hill, under the fence, and right into the cornfield. I followed after him, too hungry and thirsty to be cautious. Just as I ducked between the strands of barbed wire, I heard a voice. '¡No! ¡no! perrito. Déme el maíz.' I tried to back out and hide, but Gruff was running straight at me with an ear of corn in his mouth. And right behind him was a dark-skinned man with his grey hair pulled back in a ponytail. He saw me just as I saw him. I turned to run. He put his hand on my shoulder to stop me. I turned around and saw he was grinning ear to ear, shaking his head. 'Gringo girl,' he spoke in English now. 'Just like my granddaughter, getting into things where she doesn't belong.' He opened a canteen and poured water down his throat, then held it out to me. I took it, greedily. He looked me over head to toe. I looked self-consciously at my torn, dirty jeans and the old oversized t-shirt I'd found in the woods. 'Are you hungry?' I just nodded. 'Come on, we can use the help.' So I followed him and he gave me a basket. 'Pick tomatoes,' he said, leading me to rows of tall staked plants. He showed me how to know which ones were ripe. 'Eat one or two, no one will notice,' he whispered. I started with the cherry tomatoes, filling basket after basket, popping one in my mouth every so often. By the time I was done with the row I was full. Next I filled baskets with larger tomatoes. Gruff followed behind me, eating the tomatoes I discarded as too bruised. Then when he had his fill of tomatoes, pushing them around with his nose. At the end of the day, Javier

231

invited us back to the cabin shared by all the workers. We followed, smelling the roasting meat as we approached. They made us welcome that night and we stayed with them until November when they all went home to Mexico. All except Berta. She was a citizen, so she stayed all year around. Javier made her promise to take care of me and she did. The next spring I helped Berta plant and in June Javier and the others came back to help pick. Berta taught me a lot about plants. She also helped me get an ID. We just made up a name and a birthday and she paid a man to take my picture and print the ID. The ID said I was fifteen. Old enough to work. Not that anyone questioned the pickers. We were paid in food and cash. I never went anywhere to spend the cash."

"Why did you leave the farm?"

"It was Javier and Berta's idea. After a few years, they decided I should go to college, so they got me these books on how to pass the GED."

"You remembered how to read?"

"Not at first. But Berta and Javier both knew how to read and they showed me. After a few lessons, it all came back. After that, I read everything I could. Newspapers, novels, food packages."

"Food packages?"

"Especially milk cartons."

"Why milk cartons?"

"I thought I might see myself there and find out who I was."

"But you didn't."

"No."

The bell on Dr. Thomas' desk rang.

"Sorry, Carol. Time's up for today. Keep writing in the journal and I'll see you next week."

"Sure," Carol smiled. "It felt good to talk about Javier. I miss him."

"Seems like a good guy," Dr. Thomas smiled and waved to the door. "Bye now."

Carol was still smiling as stepped out of the office. She walked to the elevator, lost in thought. A man stood waiting for the elevator. There was something about the way he kept moving his right hand that made her nervous. She decided to take the stairs.

****

That night she had a different dream. A hand curled its fingers repetitively. Pinky, ring finger, middle finger index finger. Pinky, ring finger, middle finger index finger. First alone and then winding through her hair, tangling it, pulling, hurting. She screamed.

"Carol?" Kevin ran his hand across her forehead.

Her hand flew up and slapped his away.

"Carol, you're dreaming." He shook her lightly on the shoulder. "Wake up."

Carol started to sob. Kevin held her close and stroked her back. "It was just a dream. Everything's okay."

Eventually Carol stopped crying and fell asleep in his arms. Kevin held her, watching her face. The woman he loved had so many mysteries. He wondered if she'd ever uncover them.

****

Carol woke up when the alarm went off and wondered why her eyes felt so crusty. She hoped she wasn't getting sick. That was the last thing she needed the first month at a new job. Besides, it didn't matter. She had seedlings to repot today and they were getting crowded. Waiting until tomorrow would be a risk she wasn't willing to take. She rubbed her eyes gently and slowly opened her lids, wincing at the light. She heard the shower running. That was another way they were different. Kevin liked showers in the morning. Carol preferred a long hot bath after a day of work. Just as well. Some mornings they had a hard enough time getting out the door on time.

Carol climbed out of bed and opened the bathroom door. It was steamy from Kevin's shower, so when she looked in the mirror all she saw was a blur. She ran warm water over a washcloth and wiped her eyes. She left the bathroom and looked for jeans, a t-shirt, and a sweater. The t-shirt was for in the greenhouse. The sweater was for outside. It was cold for the middle of March. By the time she was dressed, Kevin was out of the shower. Wrapped in only a towel, he peered into his side of the closet. Carol admired the lean muscles of his back and wished they didn't have to go to work. She kissed him gently between the shoulder blades. He jumped and the towel fell to the ground.

"Sorry," Carol teased. "I didn't mean to disrobe you."

"Sure you didn't," Kevin smiled. "But I have a 9 am appointment today, so there's no time."

"I know. I have stuff to do too," Carol cast her eyes down.

"You must have had one hell of a nightmare last night."

"Why do you say that?"

"You screamed. And when I woke you up, you just cried. Don't you remember?"

So that explained the crusty eyes at least. "I don't remember a thing."

"Probably just as well," Kevin brushed her cheek with his fingers. "It seemed to be pretty terrifying."

"If it was terrifying enough to make me scream, I don't think I want to remember it."

Kevin pulled her close and hugged her, "I'll always keep you safe. You know that."

"I know," she smiled and kissed him briefly on the neck. "I love you."

"I love you too." He broke the embrace. "I'd better get dressed."

"Yeah.....and quick," she swatted his behind lightly.

****

Traffic was light and Carol arrived at work with fifteen minutes to spare. She decided to get a cappuccino and write a little in her journal. She sipped at the sweet, chocolate-dusted froth and began to write.

March 14th

Kevin said I had a nightmare last night, but I don't remember it. Maybe I block out the things that really scare me and that's why I can't remember who I am. Maybe some things are best left forgotten.

She stopped there and drank a big swallow of her coffee. She flipped the page back to the day before and read what she'd written.

235

A man with some kind of nervous twitch waited by the elevator at Dr. Thomas' building. I don't know why he bothered me, but I took the stairs.

Carol scowled at the page. It was the hand that had bothered her -- the constant repetition of the fingers.

FEAR

She wrote the word beneath yesterday's entry, and then another and another.

FINGERS

FINGER FEAR

Carol sat staring at the words on the page, her coffee getting cold, until she heard the chimes of the nearby church. She counted the chimes -- 9 o'clock. Not thinking about what she was doing, just doing it, Carol closed her journal and walked across the street to the greenhouse.

****

"What do you mean by Finger Fear?" Dr. Thomas asked a week later.

Carol shrugged, "I don't know. I guess I am afraid of his fingers."

"Or you think his fingers are afraid?"

"I guess that could be it," Carol agreed, but she knew it wasn't.

"And this man was here in the building? Do you know him?"

"No." Carol was on edge. Not only had she had the snow dream last night, but when she woke up, it was snowing and the firewood bin was empty.

"You don't want to talk about him, do you?"

"Not really."

"What do you want to talk about then?"

"I had the snow dream again last night, but it was different."

"Snow dream?"

"I haven't told you about that?"

"No."

"Oh, sorry. It's a dream I've been having forever. The snow starts falling and it covers me. Before long, I'm frozen and can't walk or talk or anything. That's when I wake up. Sometimes I have to build a fire to get warm."

"Have you ever been buried in snow?" Dr. Thomas asked.

"Not that I remember," Carol scowled. "But the dream is very real. So in a way I have."

"You said this one was different from the others."

"Yes. In this one, the snow isn't falling from the sky," Carol stacked the pencils nervously, wishing for a match. "In this one, the snow is falling from a hand."

"Like the hand of God?" Dr. Thomas asked, scribbling furiously on her pad.

"No," Carol pushed the pencils with her finger and they fell against each other, several rolling onto the floor. "Definitely not like the hand of God."

"Then whose hand was it, Carol."

Carol curled her fingers one by one, watching the snow sift through them, "Finger Fear."

The bell on the desk rang, but neither Carol nor the doctor heard it.

"Why are you doing that with your hand?" Dr. Thomas asked Carol.

"I'm not. He is."

"Who?"

"The man. He said the snow will purify me of my sins."

"What sins?"

"Not loving him."

"Was this in your dream?"

Carol looked up at Dr. Thomas, her eyes innocent and frightened. "Dream?"

"Yes, Carol. Remember we were talking about the dream you have of snow falling on you, covering you so that you can't move."

Carol's eyes grew older and she composed herself. "Yes. Usually I build a fire afterward to melt myself, but today we had no wood. Well, not in the house, anyway."

"Who was the man in your dream?"

"Man? There was no man in my dream, just a hand."

"Carol, do you ever hear or see things that aren't there?"

"No, of course not," Carol laughed nervously. "That would make me crazy."

"Have you ever been abused either physically or sexually?"

Carol cast her eyes downward, "Not that I recall."

238

Dr. Thomas looked down at the clock. "Oh my. The bell must not have rung. Your session ended ten minutes ago. Don't worry, I won't charge you for it."

Carol looked panicked. "I've got to go. I'll be late getting back to work." She slipped on her coat and grabbed her purse.

"Keep writing in the journal, Carol. And take my cell phone number just in case."

"In case of what?"

"Just in case you need it," Dr. Thomas couldn't help feeling a bit nervous as Carol Silvera walked out the door.

Carol walked to her car as quickly as she could, given the slippery sidewalk and falling snow. She couldn't believe how much snow had fallen just since she got to Dr. Thomas' office. There must be an inch or more on her windshield. She opened the door to get the snow scraper and heard a voice behind her.

"Need help? I can wipe the snow off for a dollar."

She turned and saw a young girl, no more than twelve or thirteen. Her hands were bare. "Sure. But here, use the scraper. You'll get frostbite doing it with your bare hands."

The girl shrugged and took the scraper from her. "No big deal. I do it all the time." The girl scraped the windows clean and Carol paid her two dollars instead of one. "Thanks, lady!" the girl smiled and pocketed the money. Then she ran off down the street to another car.

Carol squinted into the sunlight, watching her approach a man wiping his windshield with a bare hand. With the glare, she couldn't be sure, but she thought the man might be the one with the nervous twitch. She waited while the girl wiped his windshield clean. When the girl held out her palm for the dollar, the man motioned to the passenger-side door. As the girl walked towards the door, Carol bolted toward her screaming, "Never get in a stranger's car."

The man and the little girl looked up at her in shock.

"Are you her mother?" the man asked. "Because I didn't mean her any harm."

"No," Carol stuttered. "I'm not her mother. I just thought...Well, it's just not a good idea to get in a stranger's car. That's all."

"I wasn't going to get in his car. I'm not stupid!" the girl exclaimed.

"I had asked her to clean off my passenger and driver side windows for an extra dollar," the man said.

"Oh God. I'm sorry," Carol blushed, noticing that the man was not even the same one she'd seen by the elevator. "I completely...."

"It's okay," the man said. "I won't take offense."

The girl shrugged, "No big deal." She started swiping the passenger side window with her sleeve.

"Okay then," Carol said, still embarrassed. "Have a nice day." She walked back to her car.

****

"I really think I should stop seeing Dr. Thomas," Carol told Kevin at dinner that night.

"Why?" Kevin sliced into his steak. "Isn't she helping you remember?"

"I'm not so sure I want to remember." Carol pushed the kernels of corn around on her plate, arranging them into a circle. "Some things might be best forgotten."

"Like the nightmare?"

"Exactly."

"Well, it's your choice," Kevin looked at her and smiled. "It's not like you're crazy or something."

"No, it's not like I'm crazy," Carol grinned weakly. "I'll call her office tomorrow and let her know."

****

The next day the air was warm and the snow melted quickly. By mid-afternoon it was pretty much gone. Carol procrastinated calling Dr. Thomas all day, until finally it was too late to reach her at her office. She pulled out the card with the cell phone number, but decided against it. She'd call her tomorrow instead.

Carol walked out of greenhouse and into the nursery's retail area. Maybe she should buy a houseplant. Something cheerful for the kitchen. She chose an ornamental pepper plant and walked toward the line at the cash register. There were a surprising number of customers for the day after a snowstorm. She stood in line, noticing what the others were buying. One woman had a tray full of hardy pansies. Another balanced a tray of lettuce and chard. The man at the end of the line held a planter full of white daisies in full bloom. She thought about warning him against planting them outside this early in the year, but changed her mind. Technically she was off duty. She started to stand behind him in the line, but as she did she noticed his right hand crushing the petals of the flower it held and letting them drop, one by one to the ground. *She loves me, she loves me not.*

The man turned around and held out his right hand. In the center of the palm was a single white petal. "She loves me," he smiled, showing a gold-capped tooth. A purplish brown scar under his right eye winked at her.

Carol ran out of the nursery, forgetting she still clutched the ornamental pepper plant.

Halfway home, Carol realized she'd stolen the pepper plant. She turned around and drove back to the nursery. When she took the plant up to the counter, Angela looked at her concerned. "You bolted out of here like you'd seen a ghost."

Carol shook her head, "I don't know what I was thinking. That guy who bought the daisies ...."

"Say no more. He gave me the creeps," Angela shivered. "I think it was the eye."

"Probably," Carol tried to shrug it off. "What do I owe you?"

"With the discount, $8.29."

Carol paid and took her plant to the car. But before she got in, she looked cautiously in the back seat. Angela was right. That guy did give her the creeps.

****

"Nice plant," Kevin twirled a pepper in his fingers. "Can you eat them?"

"Technically yes, but it's really just for show."

"So, is this a hint? Are you feeling hot tonight?" He ran his finger down her spine.

"I'm always hot for you," she smiled. "Especially if a massage is involved."

"Hmmmm. We'll see," he teased.

"Okay," she looked at him with mock disappointment. "Maybe after dinner?"

"Maybe. What are you making?"

"Me?"

"I cooked last night," he said. "Steaks, remember?"

"Damn. I forgot," she opened the refrigerator door. "I was going to pick up seafood."

"Why don't we just go out?" he pushed her hand gently to close the refrigerator door. "There's a new Thai restaurant down the street I've been wanting to try."

"Works for me." The two of them left the apartment hand in hand.

It was a comfortable night and they walked to the restaurant. As they passed the alley between the music store and a dance studio, Carol held tight to Kevin's hand.

"Something wrong?" he asked.

"Nothing I can put my finger on," she replied.

"Still on edge from yesterday?"

"I guess so." She glanced over her shoulder at the young girls stepping out of the dance studio. Most walked in groups, but one girl walked alone, swinging her toe shoes from their ribbons, seemingly lost in thought. *I bet you're pretty when twirl around on your toes*, Carol heard a male voice behind her and twisted around, dropping Kevin's hand abruptly. A single old woman huddled near the entrance to a grocery store, holding out a cup for change. The young girl was gone. Carol started off running toward the alley.

"Where are you going?" Kevin ran after her.

"The girl...he can't..."

The two of them reached the alley together. It was empty, except for an alley cat digging through a trash can. Kevin put his arm around her and held her close. "What's wrong, Carol?"

"I thought..." she started to tell him about the voice, then changed her mind. "Never mind. I guess I must have just heard that alley cat yowl."

"You're sure you're alright?"

"I'm fine," she squeezed his waist. "Let's go eat some Thai food."

They walked, arms around each other, to the Thai restaurant two blocks down. The food was good and spicy, but Carol ate distractedly. And after dinner, Kevin made good on the massage, relaxing Carol and putting her to sleep. He figured she needed it and he lay next to her and watched her for a long time, glad her face looked peaceful at last. He wished he understood what was happening with her and whether talking to a psychologist was helping or making things worse.

****

"I bet you're pretty when twirl around on your toes," the man stood on the corner next to the strip mall. He had a camera in one hand and the other hung by his side, moving as if to the beat of a song. "I could take your picture."

"No thanks," the girl started to walk past him.

"Seriously," the man held out the hand that had hung at his side, a business card shook between his thumb and forefinger. "I'm a photographer. One of my customers is Dance Magazine. You've read it, right?"

The girl took the business card from the man's hand. "Of course."

"You'd be perfect for them."

"Where would I have to go?"

"Nowhere. They want some suburban shots. Dancers in a parking lot, at a bus stop, that kind of thing."

"When would you want to do it?"

"We could do it now. You're wearing your leotard under that skirt, right?"

The girl nodded her head.

Don't do it, Carol told the girl in her dream-thoughts.

"Let's get some with you putting on the shoes," the man said. "Just sit on the curb. That's nice. Now hike your skirt up a little so we can see your pretty tights. Good." The man snapped a photo. "Okay, now bend down and start putting on your shoe." He moved in closer and snapped another shot and another.

"Why do you have to get so close?" the girl asked.

"Close-up of the shoe and the ankle," he swayed a little as he squatted on the ground, placing the camera on the ground and pointing it up. "Okay, now move your hand up your inner thigh to rub your muscle." Snap. "Oops, you'd better straighten your leotard...yes...in there...a little more." Snap. Snap.

Don't you hear me? Carol screamed. *You have to walk away. Walk away now.*

The man helped the girl to her feet. "That was beautiful."

"Don't you want some pictures of me dancing?" the girl asked.

"Let's see how these turn out first," the man seemed in a hurry to leave. "Meet me at the same place next week."

Don't do it. Don't do it. Don't do it.

"Don't do what?"

Carol woke up standing next to the bed, shouting at Kevin. "Don't....I don't know. I must have been dreaming."

"Come back to bed," Kevin coaxed.

She climbed back in next to him and he wrapped his arm around her, resting it between her legs.

"Not now," she said gently. She felt dirty. "I'm going to take a bath."

"It's the middle of the night."

"I didn't get one tonight, remember? The massage oil is making me feel itchy."

"It never bothered you before."

"I know, but tonight it does," she slipped out of bed. "I won't be long."

Carol ran the water hot and scrubbed herself hard with soap and a loufa. By the time she climbed back into bed, her skin was tender, but clean. Kevin lay on his back, snoring lightly. She curled across his chest and he wrapped his arms around her. Eventually, Carol drifted back to sleep, watching pink satin toe shoes dangling from their ribbons.

Carol remembered only bits and pieces of the dream when she woke up the next morning. She wrote what she could remember in her journal. She still did not plan to go back to see Dr. Thomas, but the journal wasn't such a bad idea.

****

"I've decided I don't want to continue our sessions," Carol called Dr. Thomas from her cell phone at the coffee shop.

"Can I ask why?"

"I think there might be some things it's best not to remember," Carol saw no reason not to be honest.

"Repressed memories sometimes have a way of coming out on their own," Dr. Thomas spoke calmly. "You might not have a choice whether to remember."

"I've repressed them this long...wait, hold on." Carol saw Angela approaching quickly. "I'll call you back." She hung up the phone.

Angela slid into the chair across from Carol's, very excited about something. "Has anyone told you about the girl?"

"Girl?"

"A cheerleader went missing last night. Showed up for the game, but never went home afterward. And guess what they found in her locker?"

Carol felt the color drain from her face. "Ballet shoes?"

"Ballet shoes? Why would they find ballet shoes?"

"No reason."

"No. They found daisies. A pot of white daisies. And guess where it was purchased."

"Oh God."

"From us. The police are questioning each of us about the customers who bought daisies in the last few days. So I told them about the creepy guy. You know, the one who had you spooked, and they want to talk to you too."

"Why me?"

"You saw him, silly. You can give them a description."

"How many pots of daisies do you think the nursery sold in the past few days?"

"A bunch, but that's not the point. That guy was creepy." Angela took a sip of Carol's coffee. "Cafe Borgia's my favorite. But come on, they're waiting for you."

Carol followed Angela back to the nursery. She had mixed feelings about talking to the police. She really wanted to help them find this cheerleader, but at the same time she had to be careful not to seem crazy.

The police officer greeted her and asked her to sit down. "Ms. Carter says you saw a man buy daisies yesterday."

"Well, actually, he was standing in line. I left before he bought them."

"Can you describe the man?"

"I don't remember much. Gold tooth, scar under the right eye, and his hand..."

"What about his hand?"

"He was crushing a flower, letting it drop one petal at a time. He smiled at me and said, 'She loves me.' There was one petal in his hand. I ran." Carol gushed out the story in one breath.

"Why did you run?"

"Something about him frightened me."

"Do you know what?"

"His hand," Carol said it without wanting to.

"Was there something wrong with his hand?"

"Just the way he moved it...like this." Carol demonstrated.

"Is there anything else you want to tell us?"

Carol hesitated for a few moments, and then shook her head.

"Alright, Ms. Silvera. Thank you for your time. Here's my business card if you think of anything else."

Carol started out the door, but turned back. "There is one more thing. I think I've seen him before."

"Where?"

"I'm not sure because I only saw him from behind, but the hand moved the same way."

"And where and when did you see him Ms. Silvera?"

Carol paused again, but decided it was more important to tell. So what if they thought she was crazy. "A week ago Tuesday, waiting for the elevator on the 4th floor at 113 East Main St."

"Aren't those psychology offices on that floor?"

Carol blushed a little, "Yes...well you see..."

"There's no need to explain, Ms. Silvera. Thank you for the information."

"I just want you to find her," Carol said. "Please find her."

"We'll do our best."

Carol went back to the greenhouse and tried very hard to work. But after dropping a tray of tomato plants and knocking over a bucket of fertilizer, she decided she'd better go home. She told her manager she wasn't feeling well and left.

She wanted to go straight home, but knew she needed a few things at the store. Since they'd gone out the night before, it was her turn to cook. She walked, in a trance, down aisle after aisle, putting things in the cart she thought they might be out of. When she got to the milk cartons, she picked one up and looked at the picture on the back just like she always did. But this time, the face looking back from the milk carton was hers. "Don't go with him!" she screamed and threw the carton on the floor. She picked up another carton and looked at the familiar face on the back. "Don't do it!" she screamed. One by one, she pulled the milk cartons off the shelf, screaming at each picture, splattering milk around the aisle. The cartons changed into a pile around her...a pile of mud. Faces swam in the mud...faces she'd seen, faces she knew. A man pushed her down on the ground, and held her down next to one of others. "You want to be like that?" he screamed. "DO YOU WANT TO DROWN IN THE MUD?"

"NOOOOOO! Don't drown me!" she screamed. "I'll love you. I'll eat the roasted skin. I'll do what you want."

The man's hand wound around her hair, tangling it, caking it with mud. "Promise you'll love me?"

"Promise. I promise."

"We'll let the daisies tell us." He dragged her by the hair to a blazing fire and forced her onto a rock. Then he reached for a daisy, once white, but now brown and wilted from last night's frost. "She loves me, she loves me not, she loves me...." On and on he droned, picking petal by petal from the frost-bitten plant.

She sat silently on the rock, praying that it ended on "she loves me". Praying that his "loving" would be fast. She stared at the rocks he called Broken Heart Pass. Two green rocks, pressed together like the chambers of a heart. A streak of red rock formed a gash between them. She refused to watch his hands tear the petals off the flower.

"She loves me not!" he screamed, a single petal in his twitching hand. "SHE LOVES ME NOT." He lurched at her, but she slipped free and plunged headlong toward the fire.

She grabbed a stick from a fire and swung it around, catching him just beneath the right eye. He howled in pain. "JENNIFER! LOVE ME."

She ran into the darkness and didn't stop until the sun was red on the horizon. She found a cave nestled in the side of a hill and curled up in a ball and went to sleep. That was the last thing Jennifer remembered.

****

Carol opened her eyes and saw that she was surrounded by people, some in blue uniforms. One held a gun. Another held handcuffs. Most just stood around her, mouths dropped open. Her pants were wet and when she looked around, she saw the ruin of milk cartons and milk. "I'm so sorry," she said and started to cry. She remembered throwing the milk cartons and the faces and the....she knew who she was. She was Jennifer. Finger Fear had called her that. And Finger Fear had the cheerleader. She knew it. She motioned with her hand for an officer to come near her. The one with the gun lunged in a little closer while one of the others moved near. "Finger Fear has the cheerleader," she said.

"She's still delirious," the officer said. "Ambulance get here yet?"

"Not yet," another officer answered.

"Anyone know who she is?"

"I'm Jennifer!" she cried. "And I'm Carol."

"Alright Jennifer Carol, you're under arrest for vandalism. You have a right to remain silent..."

"I don't want to remain silent. I'm trying to tell you that I know where the cheerleader is. I know what he's doing to her because he did it to me and he did it to the faces on the milk cartons. I know what he did and what he'll do and I'll tell you if you'll listen."

"Ma'am, you'll get one phone call once we get you down to the station."

An officer put the cuffs around her wrists and led her out of the store. Jennifer watched the people gaping at her and wondered why she was in handcuffs. Carol looked at the faces on the milk cartons they passed and knew that her picture had been there many years ago.

Epilogue

Carol was taken to the police station where she was booked on the charge of vandalism. She called Kevin and got his voice mailbox. While she was waiting to try again, the officer who interviewed her walked by the cell. She told him everything she knew. He unlocked the cell and they sat in his office. He printed satellite images and maps of the forest around the farm where she'd met Javier. She worked her way through the woods to the cave she'd lived in before she was Carol, but after she'd forgotten Jennifer. Finally, she found the rocks that formed Broken Heart Pass, where Finger Fear had held her hostage. She flew with the police by helicopter, landing in a field she associated with pain and blood. They found the cheerleader not far from the field, lying in the mud, ankles and wrists bound together, clutching a bouquet of daisies. Still alive. Finger Fear was nowhere to be found.

9960859R0015

Made in the USA
Charleston, SC
27 October 2011